MURDER BY

VALENTINE

CANDY

A Novel by

Gregg Sapp

MURDER BY VALENTINE CANDY
Holidazed – Book 4
Copyright © 2021 by Gregg Sapp

FIRST EDITION SOFTCOVER
ISBN: 1622535251
ISBN-13: 978-1-62253-525-5

Editor: Lane Diamond
Cover Artist: Kabir Shah
Interior Designer: Lane Diamond

EVOLVED PUBLISHING™
www.EvolvedPub.com
Butler, Wisconsin, USA

Printed in Book Antiqua font.

BOOKS BY GREGG SAPP

HOLIDAZED
Book 1: *Halloween from the Other Side*
Book 2: *The Christmas Donut Revolution*
Book 3: *Upside-Down Independence Day*
Book 4: *Murder by Valentine Candy*
Book 5: *Thanksgiving, Thanksgotten, Thanksgone*

Fresh News Straight from Heaven

Dollarapalooza
(or "The Day Peace Broke Out in Columbus")

DEDICATION

To Laura,
a genuine lulu and my sibling in crime.

INTRODUCTION

"From your Valentine."

Sign-off in a letter from Saint Valentine to his jailer's daughter, prior to being beheaded, February 14th, 270 AD

PROLOGUE

"God bless America," Adam Erb said, placing one hand over his heart. He centered himself in front of the American flag draped on the wall behind him, looked straight into the camera, and spoke into the microphone. "And until the next time, my friends, remember: The truth ain't right or wrong. It's just true."

He then closed out by playing his theme music—a clip from "Sugarfoot Rag." When it was done, he loaded this latest segment of *Talking Truth* onto his web page, where subscribers could access it and all his other podcasts, as well as purchase T-shirts, coffee mugs, tote bags, bumper stickers, lip balm, toilet paper, and other assorted swag.

Sighing, Adam put his feet on the desk, removed his headphones, and pushed back his chair. He reached into a mini fridge on the floor beside him and cracked open a can of cold Pabst Blue Ribbon beer. He had only recently acquired a taste for it. Previously, he consumed craft ales exclusively, dismissing mass-produced lagers as "piss water." PBR still was pissy, taste-wise, but after having drank enough of it, anything else made him constipated. Besides, it wasn't like he drank PBR as a matter of taste preference; it was a lifestyle choice. According to data gathered on his website, members of his new demographic drank more

PBR than milk and water combined. He imbibed it to show that he was one of them.

Adam belched with satisfaction. It sure felt good to be back on top. He no longer took success for granted, fickle as she was. Seemingly overnight the public went from voting him the most eligible bachelor in Columbus, to reviling him as sexist and a harasser. His reputation plunged as one woman after another came forward to complain about his behavior, and, like vexing insects, he couldn't swat them away fast enough.

He never doubted himself, though. After enduring insults, hostility, accusations, and even a measure of public disgrace, he emerged on the other side with his mojo, money, and rakish good looks fully intact. He did it by remaining steadfast to his principles—that is, he denied everything, at every opportunity. Plus, it didn't hurt that he had the financial means to settle out of court. A non-disclosure agreement was a beautiful thing. Every relationship should have one. And over the long term, it was much more effective than paying ad hoc hush money to disgruntled ex-employees and bitter ex-lovers. Such was the cost of doing business.

Love was breaking out everywhere across Columbus, Ohio. Sunday was Valentine's Day, and Adam was an in-demand catch for appearances at several local venues hoping to cash in on the holiday. He checked his calendar for the next day, Friday, February 12. At 9:00 a.m. he would be the guest of honor at the breakfast meeting of the Buckeye State Babes Motorcycle Club, where the ladies would honor him with their coveted Leader of the Pack award. At 11:00 a.m., with the assistance of members of the Columbus Milk Maids roller derby team, he would cut the ribbon at the grand opening of a new Bullseye Outdoor Gear and Target

Range in Hilltop. He would then have lunch with Ginny Campbell of the WXOF News Squadron to discuss business and possibly flirt a little—Ginny didn't object to a bit of harmless dalliance. He appreciated that she was safe; although, excluding members of the press, he considered safe women a turnoff. Then, throughout the afternoon he would make drop-in appearances to hand out candy to fans at various Big Loots department stores across the greater metropolitan area. A late addition he hadn't yet put on his web page was an encore gig at Daisy Mae's Moonshiner Tavern, where he would lead the evening's first line dance. The Daisy Mae ladies loved him. With luck, maybe what's-her-name would be there again.

It was getting late. Anymore, Adam could hardly stay awake after ten. Still, before he turned in, he needed to tweet, post a story to Instagram, and add updates to Facebook. Adam never let a day go by without contributing a meme or two to the social media universe. Over the years, he'd started a veritable hit parade of hashtag trends, both before and after his personal hard times. They numbered in the hundreds, including several that peaked at number one atop Val Vargas's daily Trends You Can Use list for Columbus.

On Twitter, he tweeted, *#READY-TO-ROLL tomorrow, all over Cow Town. Can't wait to meet up with all you guys and gals. Look for me in your neighborhood. Check my website at **www.adam-erb.fan** for details.*

On Instagram and Facebook, he posted a fifteen second video of himself, shirtless beneath pinstriped bib overalls, wearing a Make America Great Again baseball cap, while he popped the hood on his custom retrofitted GMC pickup / stretch limo to check the oil level. He showed the camera that it was full, gestured thumbs up, then replaced the dipstick and dropped the hood.

He commented, *Revved up and #READY-TO-ROLL to see all my fans and valentines.*

Likes and comments began popping up in his news feed instantaneously. Adam scrolled through them, pleased by the positive reinforcement. Most responses were from fans and familiar names who cheerfully approved everything he posted. He could tweet *Eat shit and die* and they'd still love it. There were some from the usual haters too. Fuck 'em—he'd gotten the last laugh.

One posting particularly intrigued him. It read: *I'm #READY-TO-ROLL too. I'll be yours if you ride me hard.*

It was from @LadyMuleskinner—her again! He couldn't figure her out. The word *hard* contained a hyperlink. Adam imagined a curvy blond in blue jean short shorts, a plaid blouse knotted over her bare belly, pointy-toed western boots, a straw hat, and maybe a lasso or a gun belt slung over her shoulder. He couldn't resist clicking.

The link took him directly to the Erb Is a Dick website, where his enemies continued to taunt him by posting and sharing stories about how and why he was, indeed, a dick. What was wrong with those women (he assumed they were all women) that they couldn't just let bygones be bygones already?

Adam chugged the rest of his beer and crushed the can. Damn it, he couldn't let that be the last image of the day, the one he took to bed with him. He hovered his fingers over the keyboard. There were many sites he could visit to cleanse his mind and refresh his spirits. The entirety of the World Wide Web, with all its pleasures and wonders, was at his instant disposal. But for some reason he kept returning to the same damn site, where he swore every time he looked would be his last. It was like passing a car crash; he couldn't turn away. He typed in just the first two letters of the URL and his autofill finished the rest for him.

After Adam pressed Enter, his anticipation rose while the beach ball spun. The page loaded in sections. First, the banner, unrolling like a scroll to reveal the word Welcome in calligraphic script against rosé-colored wallpaper. In the center of the page was a heart-shaped padlock, with an old-fashioned skeleton key in the keyhole. By clicking on it, Adam turned the key and opened the page to an inscrutable world occupied by mostly women, but also a growing number of men, who otherwise looked perfectly normal, apart from their affiliation with SECS.

What was it? A cult, a club, a fellowship, a secret society, a conspiracy bent on world conquest? Its leader called herself Madame Secsy, and Adam distrusted her almost as much as he was curious about her. He wasn't entirely convinced that the whole SECS movement wasn't some kind of a bamboozle. If nobody was getting rich off it, then what other purpose could there possibly be for it to exist?

The group's mission statement appeared in a box across the top of the screen. Beneath it was a Join Now button. Adam had never worked up the guts to press it, not even out of purely academic curiosity. In a right-aligned column was a series of topical links, including About, FAQs, News, Who We Are, Contact Us, Schedule of Events, Testimonials, and Shop Our Site. Adam often amused himself by clicking on any or all of these links, where the content included many personal affirmations of the SECS lifestyle, replete with the kind of feel-good fluff that you might otherwise find in a Hallmark movie, but which he suspected really contained coded messages just for initiated members of the society.

Most intriguing were the personal profiles on the Meet Us link, which was limited to members only, although a handful were presented as teasers for the curious and undecided. Adam studied them carefully— Amber, twenty-eight, who had a degree in special education; Cheri, thirty-four, divorced chiropractor and mother of two; Natalie, eighteen (*eighteen! for crying out loud*), an undeclared freshman at Ohio State; and Stanley, forty-two, a patent lawyer (*wait a minute, was that Stanley—what's his name—Steadman???*) who wrote that he was "sick and tired of playing sex games" and "looking for a lasting relationship." In their profiles these people looked as normal as vanilla ice cream on white bread. But why they wanted what they wanted and, more to the point, did not want what they did not want made no sense whatsoever to Adam. They might as well not want the air that they breathe.

And yet, he was sorely tempted to join, for, deep down, he too was "sick and tired of playing sex games."

A pair of xenon headlights swept across Adam's parlor window and cast a blinding glare on his computer screen. He checked his Rolex—10:15 p.m. *What the fuck?* He went to the window and watched a black sedan approach on the long driveway and park in the turnaround at the front of his manor. Somebody got out of the car and stretched, as if arriving after a long trip.

Adam jogged to his vault room, logged onto the console of his security system, and toggled the front door camera so he could catch a glimpse of the visitor. He magnified the image on the monitor and turned on the porch lights. She faced the camera and mouthed, "Hell-o Ad-am."

"Holy Pabst Blue Ribbon," he muttered to himself. "I don't believe it."

Adam dashed into the bathroom, gargled with mouthwash, and took his special medicine. He then slipped into a pair of sweatpants, tugged on the belt of his robe, and skipped downstairs to answer the doorbell. When he reached the double doors, he squinted through the peephole, and was startled to see an eyeball look directly back at him. Adam took a deep breath and opened the door.

"Well, what a total surprise this is," he said. "You look great."

"I hope I didn't disturb you."

"Well... no, not at all. I was just checking my email."

"Can I come in?"

Adam shivered. "Uh, sure. It's cold enough to freeze a person solid out there. Can I take your coat?"

"Thanks. How about something to drink?"

"Oh? Well, sure, of course. Long island iced tea?"

"Whiskey. Straight. Pour one for yourself too."

Adam dug his hands into the pockets of his robe and pinched his thigh. It hurt, so this must be really happening. Then he wondered—can you feel pain in a dream?

"What brings you here tonight?" Adam asked.

"I have something for you. Here."

Adam accepted a heart-shaped box with a red bow on it. Although he was seldom at a loss for something to say, Adam was flummoxed. "Thanks, but...."

"I know it's a couple days early, but happy Valentine's Day."

Adam opened the box. It contained dozens of mini, multi-colored candy valentine hearts, each with a message that seemed written just for him like Kiss & Tell, Lie to Me, and Tell Me a Secret. He popped one that said R U Wet? into his mouth and sucked on it.

"Delicious," he said. "Uh, I guess I should say happy Valentine's Day to you too."

"Have another."

"Thanks, don't mind if I do."

CHAPTER 1

Jay-Rome Hawkins arrived half an hour early for the 8:00 a.m. pickup so he could turn on the heater in the Erb-mobile before his boss man was ready to roll. It took forever for that beast to warm up, and Adam Erb did not like cold. It was worth coming early if it meant giving him one less thing to bitch about.

Being early also gave Jay-Rome time to catch the question of the day on the talk radio station. If he was the designated caller and answered it correctly, he could win the grand prize of up to ten thousand dollars — although most of the time it was just tickets to a Blue Jackets game or dinner for two at Ruth's Chris Steak House. Still, if he missed a day it would invariably be the one when he could've hit the jackpot. With ten grand in his pocket, he'd feel free to tell Adam to "shove it up your Erb."

He'd always wanted to say that, but doubted he'd ever get a chance. As a convicted drug felon, Jay-Rome knew he was lucky to have any job, even one where his boss man regularly berated and demeaned him.

When Jay-Rome went to punch in the security code, he was surprised to see a smiley face on the keypad's display, indicating that the garage was already unlocked. He clearly remembered activating the security system when he'd locked up the previous day.

Something in his chauffeur's sixth sense warned him not to turn on the garage lights. Once his eyes adjusted to the dark, he could see why. The Erb-mobile's passenger windows had gossamer silk curtains drawn on all sides. Through them, Jay-Rome made out dancing blobs of greenish light—lava lamps, Adam's preferred mood lighting. Far in the back of the limo's interior, where the plush leather love seat pulled out into a queen-sized bed, Jay-Rome saw the shadowy silhouettes of two bodies, backlit by the oscillating colors. So, it looked like his boss man spent the night with a lady friend in the Erb-mobile. That happened from time to time, although when it did, he normally locked the garage behind them.

In this circumstance, Jay-Rome's instructions were somewhat at odds. On one hand, the boss man told him that he wanted to be picked up at 8:00 a.m. *sharp.* On the other hand, the boss man forbade him from interrupting whenever the silk curtains were drawn. While puzzling his next move, Jay-Rome noticed a piece of paper folded under the windshield wipers. He grabbed it and read, Donuts.

Jay-Rome grunted and shook his head. The boss man was a hog for donuts, and when he wanted them, Jay-Rome had standing orders where to get them and what to order. Before pulling out of the garage, he adjusted the rearview mirror, and saw the two shadowy figures in the back, boss man on his back, woman on top, reverse cowgirl style.

Giddyup, asshole, Jay-Rome thought.

He would've enjoyed shaking them up by taking off fast then slamming the brakes. Instead, he shrugged and eased the Erb-mobile down the long driveway and turned into the Friday morning traffic, careful not to slide on the icy road.

"*¡Ayyyyy!*" Tatiana Gonsalves squealed aloud, then whispered to herself, "He's not supposed to be here."

Huck didn't usually come on Fridays. It figured that he would change his routine on a day when she wasn't prepared. Her mother had let her oversleep. Never mind that Tati begged for her mother to leave her alone when she tried to wake her up, it was still her fault—she should have tried harder. That left Tati with barely enough time to scramble into her uniform and sprint to catch the bus, without putting on makeup, brushing her hair, or checking if the pimple on her nose had grown overnight. When she finally got to work five minutes late, her boss, Chavonne Hayes, looked her up and down and said, "Girl, yo' better get yo'self an alarm clock."

Tati worked the pickup window that morning. She glanced in the fish-eye mirror at the end of the drive-thru to count the number of cars to Huck's Prius. In doing so she made the mistake of peeking at herself in that monstrous convex mirror; it made her look like a space alien with bulging eyes and a bloated forehead. Like she should say "Take me to your leader" instead of "Welcome to Drip 'n' Donuts." The reflection stretched her nostrils wider than her mouth, and it turned that pimple into a miniature LeVeque-Lincoln Tower. It was just an optical illusion, she knew, but it made her feel like she had a freaky face not even a dog would kiss. It gave her some small consolation that the mirror also made her boobs look ginormous. With Huck's car next in line, Tati unbuttoned the top two buttons on the striped blouse of her Drip 'n' Donuts uniform.

When he pulled next to the pickup window, though, Huck failed to ogle her breasts. Instead, he had a tablet computer on his lap and continued busily entering data into yet another page of those convoluted spreadsheets he kept. He raised an index finger in the air to beg her to wait and continued punching in numbers.

Tati slid open the window as far as it could go, shimmied her shoulders all the way through, and leaned forward, so when Huck looked up he could not avoid seeing her cleavage.

"Good morning, Tati," he finally said, as if he recognized her just by looking down her blouse. If true, that was a good thing. Maybe.

"*Hola*," she said.

"How's your mother?"

"Good." Tati appreciated but also resented that Huck and her mother were friends. Their friendship gave her a reliable icebreaker when she was otherwise stuck for words. But she also worried that, in Huck's eyes, she was still just Ximena Gonsalvez's fifteen-year-old daughter. Now she was nineteen, a *woman*, old enough finally to act upon the crush she'd had on him for four years and counting.

"Did I mention that I'm taking Sociology 101 this quarter?" she asked him.

"Yes, you did."

Stupid, stupid, stupid, she thought. Of course she'd already told him—more than once, in fact. But every time she mentioned it, he gave the wrong answer. She really hoped to provoke some affirmative, mildly-suggestive comment, like "I'm glad to see you're interested in my field of expertise," or "I'd be happy to answer any of your burning questions," or "I'm conducting an experiment—would you like to volunteer?"

Barb Knoop, the new lady with an overbite and bleached blond hair, filled the bag with Huck's purchase and brought it to Tati. She looked at Tati, then at Huck, and went, "*Pfffft.*"

"Here it is," Tati said, holding up the bag for him to see. "Large coffee and one powdered-sugar donut."

"Very good," Huck said. This order was not for him. Instead, he paid it forward for the next person in line.

When he looked back at the drive-thru queue behind him, Huck's long hair fell over his brown eyes, and Tati had to put her hands in her pockets to resist the urge to reach through the window and toss it between her fingers. Huck was part Korean, which made him exotic, part fourth-generation Austrian, which made him elegant, but 100 percent corn-fed Ohio farm boy, which yielded freckles and made him, well, cute. This rare amalgam of physical features, combined with that brilliant mind of his, checked all the boxes in Tati's concept of a perfect boyfriend.

"It's almost Valentine's Day," Tati reminded him. "So, why not also pay forward a heart-shaped donut with pink icing and sprinkles? I'll tell the customer you wished them a happy Valentine's Day."

"It is? Oh. Well. That's a good idea," Huck said.

Proud of herself for having a good idea, Tati did a little dance in the pickup window.

"When they get to the widow, be sure to tell them that it's a pay it forward. Don't tell them that you know me or that it's part of an academic study. As far as they know, it's just a random act of kindness."

"Of course," Tati affirmed. She liked that she contributed to Professor Hyun-ki "Huck" Carp's research. Maybe he would mention her in the acknowledgments of his dissertation: "Special thanks to Tati Gonsalves, who helped me in so many ways."

"Good," Huck said. "I'll go park and see you in the store in a few minutes."

"I won't let you down," Tati promised him. *Just give me a chance.*

Huck's dissertation in progress contained over three hundred quantitative data points, including fifty-eight for gender alone (including eleven cis options, twenty trans choices, and, if nothing else fit, *other*, *none*, or *prefer not to answer*), and potentially hundreds of qualitative variables and indicators that he would uncover upon later content analysis of study participants' responses. His cross-sequential research methodologies included surveys, case studies, correlations, neutral observation, participant observation, secondary analysis, watching kitschy YouTube videos, and reading every issue of *O, the Oprah Magazine*.

His operational hypothesis was that pay-it-forward streaks at drive-thru windows constituted a novel socio-cognitive category of generalized exchange reciprocity wherein an emergent behavioral contagion engenders the spontaneous creation of a heterogeneous network of individuals irrespective of classical cost/benefits computations. Thus, these unplanned, purely voluntary phenomena manifest an egalitarian conception of the social commons based entirely upon an unconstrained desire of individuals to contribute to the public good. In honor of the Drip 'n' Donuts shop where he conducted his research, he referred to his theory as *donut altruism.*

He liked that idea so much it *had* to be true. Essentially, it provided a working model for organizing an overdue people's revolution against the tyranny of the 1 percent. All he had to do was prove it.

Huck didn't mention that bit about a "people's revolution" when he pitched his project for approval of the institutional research board at The Ohio State University. He was worried that the economist and the business professor on the board might veto the whole thing if it hinted of socialism. Still, in his heart Huck hoped his research would provide an outline of how to do a revolution the right way — that is, without guns, money, violence, or religion.

On randomly selected days throughout the sampling period, Huck seeded a pay-it-forward event at the drive-thru of the Drip 'n' Donuts shop on Cleveland Avenue on the north side of Columbus, Ohio. He chose that venue because he worked there as an undergraduate and was friendly with several staff members. During his employment, he participated in the great Christmas Donut Revolution of 2012: an epic twelve-hour pay-it-forward drive-thru streak that came oh so close to breaking the record for the longest ever in North America. It was a glorious thing. He ardently hoped to trigger another momentous streak, which would yield a bounty of new empirical data. And maybe break that record. It just happened that one of his sampling dates landed close to Valentine's Day. That seemed like an auspicious sign. Valentine's Day might inspire folks to open their hearts.

Commandeering a corner booth inside the shop, Huck commenced watching, listening, taking notes, and entering data. By consent of the store's manager, Huck had hooked up a workstation on a cart that he kept in a storage closet and could wheel out on days when he conducted on-the-premises research. His setup included a laptop, two monitors, a printer, a microphone to capture verbal exchanges between staff and customers, and a live link to the digital camera above the drive-thru window. When business was slow, Tati would sometimes wave or blow kisses to the camera — she was sweet, kind of silly, although Huck gently discouraged her frivolity. Neither sweetness nor silliness had any place in serious research.

Chavonne smoothed her afro braids and stepped out of the manager's office for her first morning walk-through. She had started at Drip 'n' Donuts after high school and worked nine long years on the front line before she finally got promoted to her current position. When she did, she vowed to her co-workers that, unlike the previous manager, she would be accessible to them. Accordingly, she practiced management by wandering around. Huck had suggested it to her.

Chavonne altered her gait during the walk-through, taking half steps instead of her usual long, leggy strides. It looked clumsy, but Huck suspected she did it consciously to slow down her normally brisk pace. That morning the kitchen was busier than usual. Barb on the intercom and Tati at the pickup window hustled to keep up. Chavonne looked over their shoulders and said two words she never once heard when she worked the front line: "Good job."

Upon completion of her rounds, she poured a cup of coffee and sat down next to Huck. "What up,

Professor Huck?" She pushed the coffee to him. "Got any good stuff for yo' research today?"

Huck pulled out his earbuds. "We're off to a promising start."

"I hope yo' get lots of good information today. People love them heart-shaped donuts. It's kinda cheap for a Valentine's Day present, though, if yo' ask me. Guys ought to do better by their ladies than just some cheap-ass donuts."

Huck recognized sarcasm when he heard it. "Did Eldridge get you something nice for Valentine's Day?"

"Fuck Eldridge," Chavonne snapped, then covered her mouth. "Sorry. My bad. But I done kicked Eldridge and his lazy cheatin' ass straight outta my apartment."

"That's too bad," Huck said, even though he could've predicted it. Chavonne had a poor track record with boyfriends. "He wasn't worthy of you."

Tears glazed her defiant eyes. "Blegh. Men start out worthy but can't stick to it."

Huck thought, *true that*. Sometimes he was ashamed to be male.

Since Huck personally had no romantic interest, nor immediate prospects or desire for acquiring one, Valentine's Day was inconsequential to him. He put his love life on hold pending the conclusion of his research. Suspending his sex life was a necessary sacrifice to his scholarship, although even in its absence it was sometimes a distraction.

"Hot damn," Barb cried as she looked at the drive-thru monitor. "Lookee what's a-coming. It's Mr. Talking Truth. He's the man."

Huck opened the video feed on his monitor and maximized the window for a better look. "Shit!" he cursed. "It's the goddamned Erb-mobile."

Adam Erb's one-of-a-kind limo was a remodeled GMC pickup truck, thirty-five-feet long, metallic blue, with eight doors, three axles, an 8.0-liter V10 engine, a bulldog hood ornament, and a blaster horn that played "Hang On, Sloopy." Its owner was a lot of things to a lot of people, but to Huck he was one thing above all others—a streak breaker. He was the villain who had ended the great Christmas Donut Revolution. Erb had an insatiable appetite for donuts and, although he could buy the whole Drip 'n' Donuts chain with his pocket change, he never had and never would pay forward a dime. Likewise, he discouraged his fans from participating in paying it forward. On that loathsome podcast of his, he railed against "pastry socialism" practiced by "leftist free-lunch believers," who in truth were mere pawns of "elitist deep state liberals" that hated America.

Huck pulled his hair. "Erb is the one variable that skews all of my data. He's destroying my research."

Chavonne patted Huck's hand. "Maybe he's in a mood to share some love, it bein' nearly Valentine's Day and all."

"Oh yeah, he shares the love alright—with himself." Huck bit his lip as the Erb-mobile pulled up to the kiosk. The driver rolled down his window and smiled so broadly that his earlobes wiggled.

"Welcome to Drip 'n' Donuts. How can I make your morning great?" Barb greeted him.

"Yo, yo, yo. Guh-morning to yah," he called into the intercom speaker.

The driver—his name was, what? Jerald, Jerome, no *Jay*-Rome—was always cheerful with the drive-thru staff. Huck wondered how such an amiable person could stand working for a shithead like Adam Erb.

"I got here a note from Mr. Erb, says for me to order a dozen of them jelly donuts. And to make it a baker's dozen, add a devil's food donut. That last one's for me."

"That's twelve jellies and a devil makes thirteen," Barb confirmed. "Pull up to the next window. And if you're listening, Mr. Erb, have yourself an extra special Valentine's Day."

With dwindling hope, Huck watched the Erb-mobile approach the pickup window. Tati glanced back at Huck and mouthed, "I'm sorry."

Jay-Rome stopped in front of the pickup window. Tati had the box of donuts waiting for him, as well as a large coffee.

"I didn't order no coffee," he said to her.

Tati folded her arms and said, "The last customer ahead of you already paid forward for a donut and that coffee, too. Maybe you would like to pay something forward? It'd be a nice thing to do because of Valentine's Day."

Huck appreciated that she tried; he flashed her thumbs up.

"I don't think—"

"Can't you just ask your boss?" Tati curled her lower lip and made a pouty face. "Pleeeeeze?"

Jay-Rome winced and shook his head. "Why don't you ask him when you hand him the donuts?"

Jay-Rome pulled forward so the last window at the back of the limo lined up to where Tati waited. He pushed the button to lower it.

Adam Erb's head, which had been leaning against the window, dropped and rotated faceup, half in and half out of the vehicle. Tati threw her arms above her head, knocking over the box of donuts, and screamed the kind of deranged earsplitting scream that Huck had only heard from babysitters in slasher movies.

Barb came running. When she saw inside the limo, she shrieked and vomited, hurling chunks across the span and into the Erb-mobile. "No, it ain't so!" she wailed.

Chavonne hurried to the window, took one look that made her eyes bulge, then led Barb and Tati away.

Huck pushed past the women and scurried to the window. He bent forward, with his whole upper body outside of the pickup window. He took a quick mental snapshot.

Adam Erb's nearly nude corpse was as flat and rigid as an ironing board. His purplish skin stretched so tight it looked like it might tear like tissue paper.

Someone had inscribed #pERBvert in black marker across his chest.

He wore a hard shell helmet, a Lone Ranger face mask, a bow tie around his neck, and skull-and-crossbones rings on both his middle fingers. A yellow rose rested under his chin.

He was handcuffed behind the back. His fists were jammed with Monopoly money.

He wore calf-high cowboy boots, left on right and right on left.

He wore a leather belt with a chain-mesh trap covering his genitals and secured by a keyed padlock. The mesh strained to hold back a monolithic erection.

Ouch, Huck thought.

His mouth and cheeks were packed with heart-shaped sugar candies, which spilled from the corner of his mouth onto the crook of his shoulder, his lap, and the seat all around him. They bore printed messages like Be Nasty, Spoiled Rotten, Spank Me, Bad Boy, I Like It Rough, and other mildly sadomasochistic suggestions.

Lying next to him was a frighteningly realistic elastomer sex doll, with full red lips, D-cup breasts with hard rubber nipples, a vulcanized vulva with pink latex labia, and one hand suctioned onto Adam Erb's ass.

On the floor was a stogie cigar, an assault-style squirt gun, several crushed cans of Pabst Blue Ribbon, and a cell phone. Looking closer, Huck noticed a matchbook from the Booti Tooti Club wedged into a crack between seats.

Jay-Rome got out of the car and stopped cold in his tracks. "I, uh, oh shit, uh, fuck, I'm, uh, ick," he stammered. "God*damn*."

"Call 911!" Chavonne cried.

"Tell them there's no hurry." Huck reached forward to close Adam's eyelids. "He is so dead."

CHAPTER 2

Huck took charge of securing the crime scene. First, he directed Chavonne to close the drive-thru and request customers to remain there until the police arrived.

"Why for am I s'posed to tell them?" Chavonne asked.

"Tell them that we're having, uh, technical difficulties," he suggested.

"Uh huh. That's what we got. A corpse with technical difficulties."

Next, he sent Barb to find something to use in lieu of police tape to establish a perimeter. She came back with a string of Christmas lights they had just put away after the holidays.

Huck looked at them. "That will do. Now, wrap them around the entire drive-thru, from the entrance in the parking lot to the Thanks and Come Again sign at the end."

Meanwhile, Jay-Rome paced back and forth in front of the Erb-mobile. "I was just driving and didn't even look back there. I sure 'nuff didn't know he was dead. If I did, I ain't never have taken him to get donuts. You'll do believe me, right?"

Huck placed his hands on both of Jay-Rome's shoulders. "Go inside and sit down. Have a donut."

"Yeah, yeah, yeah. Sure." Jay-Rome kept talking to himself as he walked away. "He was a shitty boss who dissed me every chance he got, but ain't nobody deserves to die in such a gnarly way like that."

Once he got everybody out of his way, Huck returned to the limo for a closer look. The body was as rigid as a steel rail, swollen, and channeled with dark, protruding veins. It looked like he'd been drained of blood and given a transfusion of silicon carbide. This was more than just rigor mortis. Huck took one of the candy pieces and sniffed it. Every piece was the same shade of pale blue, and upon breaking one apart, he realized that instead of a solid heart-shaped nugget, the candy contained two smooth diamond-shaped pills, adhered together with sugar and gelatin. The back side of each pill was etched with VGR 100. The primary ingredient of the candy hearts was a high dosage of sildenafil, aka Viagra. It looked like Adam's murderer had handcuffed him, perhaps consensually at first, then fed him the candy, again possibly in some manner of kinky foreplay, but faster and in greater number until he couldn't swallow fast enough to keep from choking. Meanwhile, under the influence of a massively overdosed priapism, his veins turned to stone. The corpse of Adam Erb was a whole-body erection.

Whoever did this must be severely psychopathological, Huck thought, with begrudging admiration.

The perp had left clues. Huck recognized the lock and key on the chastity belt as the logo of the Society of Enlightened Celibate Savants (aka SECS—pronounced SEX). In Huck's informed opinion, the Society represented a rejection of the hypersexualization of, well, *everything* in modern American culture. Intellectually, it had some merit. In practice, though, the society's austere membership requirement was difficult to sustain and almost ensured diminishing returns. Huck suspected it attracted people who likely wouldn't get laid, anyway. It most certainly was not for the likes of Adam Erb.

Huck lifted Adam's cell phone from the limo floor. Its screen was unlocked. Two windows were open — one was his to-do list for that day, and the other was the feed on Adam's personal web page, which included hundreds of comments related to his last podcast. Huck scrolled through them. Many offered acclamations, like *Kudos, Right on, Damn straight, Fuckin' A,* and *Ain't it the truth?* Others were hostile, like *Fuck you and eat shit,* and some were downright vicious, such as *Castration is too good for you* and *Up your ass with a power drill.* One particularly stood out from all others for its ambiguous message; it was from @LadyMuleskinner, and it said, *You'll get what you deserve in the end.*

Somebody bumped Huck from behind. He pivoted, hands in the air, as if in surrender.

Tati jumped back. "Whoa. Sorry if I scared you."

Huck perked his ears at the sound of approaching police sirens. "Do you have your cell phone? Can I borrow it?"

She handed it to him guardedly. "What for?"

Huck immediately started taking photos of the corpse, the interior of the limo, and screen shots from Erb's cell phone. When he gave her back the phone, he asked, "Please, Tati, can you email these pictures to me?"

"Right away. Don't you worry. You can count on me."

"Thanks." He gently nudged her away. "Now go inside. The police will be here soon."

With that, Huck tucked in his shirt and combed his hair with his hand. He stood guarding the Erb-mobile while three police cars, an ambulance, and a sport utility vehicle with a flashing light on the dashboard pulled into the parking lot in front of Drip 'n' Donuts.

"Adam fucking Erb," Detective Sally Witt grumbled as she hoisted herself out of her Land Rover. She was hardly shocked that somebody had murdered him. A lot of people hated his guts. Whoever had Erb in the office death pool had just won a nice sum.

After her first ten years on the Special Victims Bureau of the Columbus Police Department, Detective Witt thought that she'd seen it all. At least she'd hoped so. For utter, audacious depravity, she once thought that nothing could beat the Obetz baby pacifier butt plug pornographer or Eli the Amish farmer's market eggplant masturbator. But after twenty years on the force, she had come to begrudgingly accept that the human capacity for creative lechery surpassed any of her most vile imaginings.

Her colleagues on the force were wrong when they called her hard-hearted. No, hers was completely petrified. Twenty grueling years with SVB had led her to three inescapable conclusions: all men were venal, filthy swine; the only justice was revenge; and happy endings existed only in fairy tales, romance novels, and Asian massages.

The Drip 'n' Donuts where Erb's body was found occupied a corner at a strip mall in a seedy neighborhood in north Columbus, where Crips and

Bloods both claimed territory, and violent skirmishes often erupted over gray areas. Still, the gangs generally left the donut shop alone because it was a popular place for cops to grab a quick cup of coffee and a pastry. Detective Witt herself had occasionally patronized the drive-thru. Donuts and coffee were staples at a stakeout.

Already, despite no official confirmation, social media buzzed about the murder of Adam Erb. The ensuing fracas around the donut shop looked like a flash mob collided with a traffic jam. A dozen cars were parked in the drive-thru, while their drivers and passengers milled about, gabbing and jostling with each other, and damn near every one of them was taking a cell phone video. Gossips and gawkers packed the sidewalk in front of the store. Traffic stopped completely in one lane of Cleveland Avenue. Adding to the confusion, there were two perimeters — one plotted by the police and demarcated by yellow Do Not Cross tape, and a second wider region contained within strings of blinking multi-color Christmas lights that encompassed the entire shop, drive-thru, and parking lot. Cops guarding the crime scene got their feet tangled in extension cords and, in trying to extricate themselves, yielded ground to the mob.

The Erb-mobile was at the center of the melee. Forensic lab geeks poked and probed the vehicle to gather evidence. Detective Witt elbowed her way to the front and shoved aside a geek to get a look at the body. Corpses were nothing new to her. She'd seen her fair share of blood, viscera, and mutilation, which had no more effect upon her than a bug splattered upon a windshield. Nevertheless, seeing Adam Erb stone cold dead, bloated, and contused in the backseat of his limo triggered an unexpected gag reflex. In some of her darker fantasies, she'd imagined his demise, even secretly wished for it as a kind of karmic justice. Many times, she'd wanted to punch his smarmy smirk off his face. Now, unable to avert her gaze from the frog-like contortions of his distended cheeks and twisted brow, she was surprised by a surge of syrupy acid reflux rushing into her mouth. She spat it onto the curb.

"Gross, ain't it?" The geek sounded titillated.

Gross hardly did it justice. This case was over the top in several paraphiliac categories, and maybe some new ones too. "What happened here?" Detective Witt asked.

"Can't say for sure until we get the body to the lab, but just eyeballing it, I'd wager he suffered a fatal coronary due to a massive overdose of erectile dysfunction medication."

"Are you shitting me?" Detective Witt tried not to sound amused. It could not have happened to a worthier person. "He died of a hard on?"

"Not exactly, but, maybe, yes. Each candy heart contains two hundred milligrams of sildenafil. It looks like he swallowed dozens of them."

The geek picked up one of those hearts with a tweezer and held it for Detective Witt to read. Its little message was, Eat Me.

Detective Witt groaned and left the geek cackling like a teenage boy who'd found his father's hidden porn. She walked the length of the Erb Mobile, at once admiring it and disgusted by it. The limo was bigger than her living room and had nicer furniture. The sound system alone was probably worth more than her single-wide mobile home. It was a playboy mansion on wheels. She kept her mind from straying by reminding herself that this was the scene of a brutal murder. That helped.

Nearby, Adam Erb's chauffeur pleaded with a uniformed cop. "I ain't done nor seen nothin.' Somebody done set me up for this."

"Did you discover the body?" the detective stepped in and asked him.

"Nuh uh. They done saw it before me." He pointed at the donut shop staff.

Detective Witt went to them. "Who's in charge?"

Three women huddled together next to the drive-thru kiosk. One of them, whose name tag read Chavonne, replied, "I'm the manager."

"Excuse me, please," a young man interrupted. He was tall and scrawny, with long stringy black hair in his eyes; he looked to be of mixed race. "I was the first person to examine the body."

"You did *what?*" Detective Witt blurted out.

"Only in a cursory manner, of course. I left everything intact. But I took notes. I'm happy to share them with you."

"Leave the police work to us, Sherlock," she said.

"Well, yes, about that... I really think you should extend your crime scene boundary to include the area I marked off with Christmas lights."

Detective Witt snorted and pinched her eyes. "Who in the hell are you?"

"My name is Hyun-ki Carp. Everybody calls me Huck. I'm a doctoral student in social psychology at Ohio State, so I know a thing or two about forensic sociology."

"Oh, do you? Please, enlighten me."

"Clearly the killer had a reason for staging the body in this manner and delivering it here to be discovered.

If you want to understand the killer's motives, you must consider the demographic entirety of the crime and its socioeconomic victimology."

Fuck me, Detective Witt thought. An amateur sleuth was a special type of crank, one who thought he was smarter than the cops.

"Yeah. Right," she growled at Huck. She turned to Chavonne. "I'm going to need you and your staff to give statements to our officers." She knotted her brow and looked directly into Huck's eyes. "Especially you, Professor Carp."

"Of course. I will look forward to it."

"Uh huh," Detective Witt mumbled. *What a rube*, she thought.

A clamor arose from the crowd and distracted the detective. Horns honked, feet stomped, hands clapped, and people made room for two cargo vans to pass through. The first vehicle parked next to a snowplow pile across from the donut shop entrance; the other blocked the exit of the drive-thru. Crews of technicians poured out of both vans and began setting up separate bases of operation, with lighting, booms, satellite dishes, and other elaborate telecommunications equipment. Last out of each van were two fashionably dressed women, each carrying a microphone and followed closely by a camera person.

"Shit," Detective Witt said. "Here come those goddamned barracudas from the press."

D'Nisha Glint came into the WCBN studio uncharacteristically early that day. It was nearly Valentine's Day, and she needed a suitably romantic and/or sensational story for the occasion, like long lost lovers reunited and/or murdered. She logged on to her tip line. It continually amazed her how her followers were instantly on top of any and all newsworthy events anywhere in the ten counties of the central Ohio region. She was an investigative reporter, sure, but they did a lot of the actual investigation for her, leaving her to concentrate on work in front of the camera, where she was at her best.

By midmorning, the in-basket for her *Eyewitness Accounts* blog overflowed with urgent messages on some variation of the subject ERB. This was far from the first time that her followers had flooded her with information concerning her ex-boyfriend and current antagonist, Adam Erb. D'Nisha appreciated how they kept an eye on him, so she didn't have to. Dirt on Adam Erb was like money in the bank. On that day, though, her sources reported that Adam was *dead*, under highly unusual and suspicious circumstances.

This was the story she dreamt of!

D'Nisha checked her face in the mirror, did some quick touch up with eyebrow liner, dusted the sides of her face with bronzer, and applied deep crimson lipstick to add a touch of feminine gravitas to her features. Finished, she kicked back her chair and called, "Let's roll!" to her mobile news crew. Her camera person and two technicians knew the drill; they loaded the van and picked her up in front of the building in five minutes flat.

"What took so long?" D'Nisha scolded them.

The WCBN van passed traffic on Cleveland Avenue as it sped toward the Drip 'n' Donuts in north Columbus. It irritated D'Nisha when other drivers refused to yield — so far as she was concerned, the news van was every bit as much of an emergency vehicle as an ambulance. Getting to a story first gave her the right of way. Thus, seeing another vehicle in the rearview mirror gaining on them angered her. Even worse, it was the WXOF News Squadron van.

"That's Ginny fuckin' Campbell," D'Nisha cried. "Don't let that bitch get there before us," she ordered her driver.

The race was on. Northbound on Cleveland Avenue, both vehicles sped neck and neck from Weber Road to Oakland Park Avenue, where the light turned yellow as they approached. Neither had time to make it before the light turned red.

"Don't you fuckin' dare stop," D'Nisha commanded.

The WCBN van hurtled through the intersection three full seconds after the light turned red, eliciting a salvo of honking horns and middle fingers from drivers. Meanwhile, the WXOF van skidded to a halt behind them.

"Eat my scoop!" D'Nisha shouted back at the competition.

The advantage was short-lived, however, for traffic bottlenecked on Cleveland Avenue in front of the Drip 'n' Donuts shop. The WCBN van bulldozed through the logjam, but in doing so led interference for the one from WXOF, which had quickly caught up. They both parked after pressing forward as far as they could go. D'Nisha and Ginny hopped out of their vans simultaneously. They sneered at each other, then hastened to the crime scene as if the police tape were a finish line.

D'Nisha accosted a burly woman wearing reflective shades and a black peacoat, with a badge on her belt. "Is it true that Adam Erb is dead?"

Ginny followed up with, "Was he murdered?"

"I'm Detective Sally Witt." The woman lowered her shades. "I can confirm that the victim, Mr. Adam Erb, is deceased. The matter is under investigation. Other than that, the Columbus Police Department has no further comment." She turned, cracked her knuckles, and skulked away.

That's what the police always say, D'Nisha thought. *But there is more than one way to get a story.*

D'Nisha scanned faces in the crowd. Three women wearing the Drip 'n' Donuts uniform stood around the drive-thru kiosk as if they faced a firing squad. She quickly sized them up—one, a doe-eyed young Latina was cute but had a monumental zit on her nose; the second, a plump straw-haired blond, chewed her fingernails like she ate corn on the cob; and the third, a striking black woman, wagged her finger while having an animated conversation with a police officer.

That's the one, D'Nisha thought. *Sistah!*

"Follow me," D'Nisha barked to her camera person, whose name she'd forgotten. She grabbed a microphone and pointed it at the *sistah.* "Ma'am, please. Will you speak with the press?"

"Who me?" she asked.

"Yes, you. Come to me."

Chavonne complied, ducking under the police tape. "Aint yo' D'Nisha Glint?"

"I am. And you are?"

"Chavonne Hayes. I've done watched yo' on TV since yo' did the weekend weather reports. Yo' look taller in real life."

"That's so sweet," D'Nisha said. "What happened here?"

"When the limo pulled next to our pickup window, that Erb dude was dead as a brick and hard as one, too."

"Great! I mean, that sounds awful. Can I interview you for the WCBN news?"

Chavonne smiled for the camera. "Hell yes!"

"Fantastic!"

D'Nisha pulled what's-his-name the camera person forward by the collar of his T-shirt, hard enough to snap back his head and nearly cause him to swallow his cigarette. D'Nisha tsked. "Oh come on. We're going live."

D'Nisha positioned herself to favor her better side. The camera person hoisted the EFP camera onto his shoulder and commenced counting backward from five. At one, D'Nisha steeled her features and spoke in the grim voice she reserved for reporting on murder, sex crimes, and losses by The Ohio State football team.

"Hello, Columbus. This is D'Nisha Glint reporting from the Drip 'n' Donuts on the north side of Columbus, where one of the city's most infamous and controversial figures has met with a grisly fate. Columbus police confirm that *Adam Erb* — the business mogul and socialite, who recently was the subject of numerous sexual harassment allegations — has died under suspicious circumstances. I have with me Ms. Chavonne Hayes, manager of the Drip 'n' Donuts shop, who found Mr. Erb's body in the drive-thru. What did you see, Ms. Hayes?"

Chavonne cut loose. "Let me tell you, D'Nisha—can I call you D'Nisha? Anyhow, that Erb dude wasn't just dead, he was messed up nasty. In the back of that kick-ass limo, he was all purple and swollen, with little bits o' valentine candy crammed down his throat. And he was all butt nekkid, except for some kinda metal jockstrap squeezing all his junk. It was sick."

D'Nisha thought, *Perfect.* There was nothing like a naked dead celebrity to propel her ratings through the sky.

While D'Nisha interviewed Chavonne, Ginny Campbell searched the crowd for an eyewitness of her own. She looked for somebody with whom her audience could relate, preferably a woman, even better, one who looked bedraggled and emotionally overwrought. Best of all was a weeper, and Ginny found one. A dirty blond with crooked teeth, dressed in the Drip 'n' Donuts uniform, stood with her back to the drive-thru kiosk, gnawing anxiously on her knuckles as if holding back a deluge of tears.

"Follow me," Ginny said to Troll, her camera dude.

"Where you lead, I will follow," Troll replied.

While Ginny pushed through the crowd, she got thumbs ups and friendly slaps on the back from several onlookers. The working-class, salt-of-the-earth folks from the north side were her kind of people, God bless them.

The blond with the crooked teeth removed her hand from her mouth when she realized that Ginny was heading straight for her. She looked like she might bolt.

"Wait!" Ginny called to her. "Speak to me. *Please.*"

Ginny was a master of using the word *please*; few could refuse her, not even Adam Erb, God rest his soul. The blond woman stuffed her hands in her pockets and sunk her head between her shoulders, like a schoolgirl who hadn't done her homework.

Ginny said to Troll, "Start with a wide shot to get the crowd, then move in for a closeup if she starts bawling."

"Check. Zoom on the waterworks."

"Hi," Ginny said when she reached the woman. "I'm Ginny Campbell."

The woman's lower lip quivered. "I know," she said. "I watch you on WXOF."

"That's so kind of you," Ginny replied. "May I ask your name?"

"My name is Barb. Barb Knoop."

"Barb! Well then, you work here, don't you?"

"That I do."

Up to this point, Ginny had concealed the microphone in her coat pocket. She removed it and thrust it in Barb's face before she could object. When the little red light on Troll's camera flashed solid, she began: "This is Ginny Campbell, live from the scene of the apparent murder of one of this city's most influential voices. Adam Erb, the entrepreneur and host of the popular podcast *Talking Truth*, is dead. Detectives are not releasing any details. But I have here Barb Knoop, a witness who works at the Drip 'n' Donuts where his body was found. Please be advised that some of the details may upset sensitive viewers. Ms. Knoop, can you tell me what you saw?"

"Are we on TV now?" Barb asked

"Yes, ma'am. What can you tell me about today's incident?"

Barb leaned into the microphone so close that Ginny could smell her breath, which reeked of tuna fish.

"Well, I got excited at first when I saw Mr. Erb's limo pull into the drive-thru. I'm a big fan of his. I even met him once. When the limo stopped at the pickup window, I went to say howdy. But he was already dead."

"I'm sorry. I know this is difficult to talk about. But what did you see?"

"It was gross. I don't know how somebody could do such a thing. It was probably one of them feminazis that wouldn't give him no peace, when all he ever did was tell the truth."

While listening to Barb expound upon the shocking particulars of Adam Erb's demise, Ginny conjured a solemn expression with her eyes, but also stiffened her cheeks, which she hoped her viewers would see as grief tinged with outrage.

Barb wrapped up by saying, "Whoever done this ought to be hanged dead." Then she sniffed, her cheeks deflated, her brow knotted up, and she began weeping as if her eyes had burst open.

Perfect, Ginny thought.

CHAPTER 3

"I've never seen anything like this," Val Vargas said to her favorite cat, Minou. The cat looked up from her perch in the windowsill and yawned.

Nobody knew Internet trends like Val. She had influenced nearly all the greatest trends in Columbus social media history. Her fame as a networking guru began back in 2012, when she almost single-handedly launched the great Christmas pay-it-forward streak at Drip 'n' Donuts by tweeting: *Instant karma! Pay it forward at N Cols D&D. Share sum Xmas <3. #FEEDtheDEED.*

#FEEDtheDEED henceforth became a rallying cry for random acts of kindness across Columbus, and Val was its undisputed creator. From that humble beginning, Val's career took off like "Gangnam Style." She modestly believed she could pick any random word in the dictionary, attach a hashtag to it, post it on Twitter, and magically start a new trend.

What she witnessed that morning, though, was totally unprecedented. Across all social media platforms, conveyed through a variety of hashtags, manifested in half a dozen major trends, there was only one topic of discussion online throughout the entire central Ohio region. The first wave began around nine, when several news services reported that Adam Erb had died. Val immediately suspected that this story had legs, but what happened next was beyond her wildest 5G fantasies.

Soon thereafter, Twitter exploded with tweets, retweets, and after tweets, conveying every possible opinion about Adam Erb, dead or alive. Meanwhile, images of Erb popped up everywhere—some of which were reposted, cut and pasted, or outright plagiarized from sites all over the Web. Soon, photos purportedly taken at the scene of the crime appeared on Instagram, Flickr, and Snapchat, followed by videos popping up on YouTube and Twitch. An Erb subreddit site emerged out of nothing. A Facebook group became the de facto clearinghouse of all things Erb.

From her home headquarters overlooking the Scioto Mile Promenade, Val watched the whole online epic unfold in real time. The living room of her penthouse condo contained wall-to-wall desks stacked with the components of a broadband local area network, including a router, two servers, six computers, and a dozen monitors, which worked in concert to catalog and quantify diverse social media activity. Val sat at the central command hub in front of an enormous monitor, where she could keep track of every stream, blog, meme, board, slogan, tweet, keyword, and hashtag, which collectively provided raw data on the hottest local topics of that day, hour, and minute. Her systems tagged all pertinent data, which she then ran and compiled through a nexus analyzer, and—*voila!*—the result was the most comprehensive readout of local social media trends, distilled and ranked for quick consumption. For a nominal subscription price, she shared this information through her for-profit website, VV's Trends You Can Use.

Although Val considered her work an essential public good, she saw nothing wrong with taking well-deserved remuneration from the proceeds. The overhead costs were considerable, not the least of which was the 24/7 demands on her personal time. Even a labor of love had to pay the bills.

Based upon her unrivalled expertise, Val could usually predict the lifespan of any trend. Few lasted twenty-four hours before flaming out. The Internet had a short attention span, but a long memory. This Erb tsunami of online activity went from zero to the highest peak she'd ever seen in a single hour, and it was still gaining momentum. It bounced around from person to person to person, then back again, modified at each turn enough to make it new all over again. There was no guessing how, when, or even *if* it might end.

Val was excited to be the gatekeeper of such an astonishing phenomenon, but she was also humbled by the responsibility. This was uncharted social media territory. What if she missed something? Although she understood trends better than almost anybody, this was an anomaly unlike anything in her extensive online experience. It violated the laws of Internet physics. How could she wrap her head around it?

If she knew anybody qualified to help, it was Huck. He was a genius. He knew what you were going to do or think even before you did it or thought it. Although it had been a couple years since they'd been in touch, she knew he would jump at this opportunity to make history with her. Val texted to him, *Dead Erb = hyperviral! U'll want 2 see this. Call me.*

Tati insisted on tagging along. Despite initial misgivings, Huck agreed to let her accompany him on his visit with Val. As Tati pointed out to him, Val was more her friend than his. That was a valid point. Additionally, Huck realized he didn't have any legitimate reason for excluding her, apart from some vague feeling she would distract him. Sometimes Tati's presence made it hard to concentrate.

"It's been too long," Val said to Huck when she opened the door. She kissed him on both cheeks. He restrained the urge to wipe them off.

Val wore a terry cloth robe and slippers. She had colored her hair a blinding new color, something like neon tangerine. Huck felt like good manners dictated he should tell her she looked good, but he worried that saying so would sound insincere, because she looked to him like she had Cheetos for hair.

Tati stepped forward and opened her arms wide. "Hey, girlfriend—¿Cómo estás?"

"Hugs and kisses," Val replied.

They embraced and giggled, as if tickling each other. Huck bounced on his feet, waiting for them to cease their effusion of silliness. When they finally separated for a breath, they started giggling all over again, then lunged back for more hugs.

A red-and-white piebald cat rose, stretched, jumped down from the windowsill, and brushed against Val's calves.

"Hey, you've got a new cat," Tati observed.

Val picked it up, stroked behind its ears, and said, "This is Minou. She's not just any cat. She's my feline soul mate."

Something about that remark sent Tati into further paroxysms of giggling, which triggered more of the same from Val.

Huck checked his watch. Time was wasting. He left them to get the giddy nonsense out of their systems, while he went exploring in Val's condo. Its décor was a cross between a teenage girl's bedroom and a military command bunker.

A plush blue velvet sofa was piled with pillows, stuffed animals, and oversized blankets. Huck counted four more cats lounging in tiny beds — actual beds, with box springs, mattresses, and headboards. Other furniture created just for the cats included hanging windowsill perches, climbing towers, and miniature outhouses containing litter boxes.

By contrast, Val's workspace blinked and buzzed with multiple high-tech devices. Workstations were equipped with an array of computers and monitors, three rolling ergonomic chairs, a tangle of cables tied together and plugged into four surge protectors on the floor, and a cabinet with shelves containing printers, speakers, a camera, a scanner, a plotter, a projector, and spare parts. Centered above it all, a giant eighty-five-inch ultra-high-definition flat-screen monitor hung on the wall. Its screen flashed with indecipherable strings of rapidly scrolling code. Huck felt stupid because he couldn't make sense of any of it.

On their way to rejoin Huck, Val grabbed a box of peanut butter chocolate chip cookies and popped one in her mouth.

"Cookie?" she asked.

"No, thanks. I'm watching my weight," Tati replied.

Val frowned.

"Don't mind if I do," Huck said, taking one from the box.

An alarm went off on one of the computers. "OMG," Val cried. She barreled between Huck and

Tati, scooted in front of the nearest keyboard and frantically began punching in a command. When she hit Return, the giant monitor on the wall showed the image of a steeply curved graph with about a dozen colored trend lines superimposed on top of each other and plotted against an x axis listed as "time" and a y axis, "posts."

"Look," Val said. "There's a new number-one-trending hashtag. It's #MurdERB. This is the second time it's peaked today. Others currently making up the top five are #pERBvert, #HatERB, #ExacERBated, and #MartyrERB. Those are just the top five, there are around a dozen more. Everybody has something to say about Adam Erb. He pushes all of people's hot buttons — sex, money, celebrity, scandal, politics. People love him. People hate him. Heck, once I loved him, then I hated him, then started to almost love him all over again. He once emailed me that he considered my daily trends list to be *indispensable*. I mean, wow! After that, it was the least I could do to help him design his website."

"Personally, I never changed my mind about him. He was always a loathsome capitalist," Huck said.

"He was good looking, but totally creepy," Tati added.

"My point exactly!" Val pounced. "Can you imagine what would've happened if there had been social media when Elvis died? This is like that. Look here...."

Val keyed in a new command. The giant monitor blanked out for a moment, then returned with a multicolored branching graph. "This is a model of how one trend spread, from its first posting under the hashtag #HypERBole, through cycles and clusters as people replied to it, shared it, changed it, added to it, commented on it, trolled it, ghosted it, reposted it, and linked to it. Each point of contact became a new data tree. Trends need to be fed. Usually, their roots peter out, and the whole tree collapses. But just imagine if one didn't. What if a trend continued to spin off brand new branches, and those took off on their own too, and so on? It would be like immortality."

Tati stepped forward, slack-jawed, with her nose inches from the giant screen. "Can you use all this to peep at people through their computers?"

"Hmmm," Val pondered. "I might actually be able to do that."

"But you wouldn't, like, look into people's bedrooms, right?"

"Of course not!" Val asserted. "I respect people's privacy. Even when they don't deserve it."

Huck marveled at how far Val had come in the five years since he worked with her at Drip 'n' Donuts, where she continually peeked at Facebook on her phone while watching the counter. Back then, he considered her somewhat of a dim bulb. Maybe that's why she excelled as a social media influencer.

"This is an amazing setup," Huck said to Val. "I wish I had half this much computing power for my research."

"That's why I called you. These trends are unlike any that I've ever seen. Usually, a trend launches, tops out, falls, then disappears. But here, new hashtags are spinning off into baby hashtags. They are talking to each other and, well, *reproducing*. It's kind of like they are paying it forward. It reminds me of our amazing streak, back when we both worked at Drip 'n' Donuts."

"True that," Huck said.

"I was there too," Tati reminded them.

As Huck recalled, Tati was only there because her mother, Ximena, worked at Drip 'n' Donuts. She hadn't actually participated, being just a kid at the time.

"Anywho," Val continued, "I'm puzzled. I've never seen trends behave like this."

Huck sat down at one of the workstations and studied the data stream. "This is fascinating. It looks to me like memes are being diffused via weak networks across multiple nodes."

"Huh?" Tati asked.

"Whatever," Val said. "But the point is that you can, like, explain to me how this is happening. Right?"

"I will have to study the data," Huck replied.

Val bounced up and down on her toes and clapped her hands. "You want data? You got data! It's all yours."

"Thanks." Huck pushed back in the chair. "But tell me—what's in this for you?"

Val cradled her arms like holding an infant. "It's like watching the birth of a new species. I want to see how long I can keep it going. Just like your pay-it-forward streaks. I think I can break the world record."

"¡Órale!" Tati cried. "They keep records of such things?"

"Duh. They keep records of everything," Val answered.

Huck stood transfixed in front of the giant monitor; it felt like trend lines ran in one ear and out the other. "I can't make any guarantees," he said. "There are multiple variables to consider. But I'll crunch the numbers and see what I can come up with. There may be trends within trends that nobody has ever detected."

"I'll help," Tati volunteered. "I'm good with numbers."

Rather than acknowledge Tati, Huck addressed Val. "I have something else I would like to ask you."

"OFC, Huck. Ask and ye shall receive."

"What do you know about SECS?"

Tati jabbed Huck with her elbow. "No, no, no," she admonished him. "You can't just up and ask a lady about such things."

Val: "I don't know much about sex, anyway."

Huck: "Let me be more specific. I was asking about the Society of Enlightened Celibate Savants."

Tati's jaw dropped. "Does that mean, like, they don't *boom chicka boom boom*?"

Val bristled. "Why are you asking me about them?"

"I just figured, well...."

Val plopped down onto her sofa and tugged on the cords of her robe. "That's okay. I get it. You know me. I stay home with my cats and my computers. I don't have much time to date. So, I found out about SECS about a year ago. We meet online. Most of the guys I've FaceTimed are fun, and since sex is off the table, there's no pressure."

"That's so sad," Tati jumped in. "But, hey, I got a cousin you might like. He's *mucho caliente*."

"Thanks, but no thanks. Celibacy works for me," Val said to Tati, then turned to Huck. "Why do you ask? Are you thinking about joining?"

"No, he's not," Tati butted in.

Huck glanced at Tati from the corners of his eyes, trying to convey both surprise and rebuke. "Not right now," he said to Val. "I was just curious if there has been any buzz from the Society about Adam Erb."

"Oh, sure," Val replied. "The very first number one hashtag was #pERBvert. It began with an anonymous tweet on the Erb Is a Dick website, but it really took off when @MadameSECSY tweeted, *Adam #pERBvert is proof that sex kills.*

"The hashtag was #pERBvert?"

"Yes. It skyrocketed to the top of the trends list."

"About what time was it posted?"

"It was a little after eight. I know because I'd just finished my online yoga class."

Huck plugged this information into his developing timeline. At eight, Erb's limo was just pulling into the drive-thru at Drip 'n' Donuts. So, when and how did @MadameSECSY—or whoever managed the Erb Is a Dick website—learn that he had died? Additionally, the #pERBvert hashtag scrawled on the body was never made public. That could not have been a coincidence.

Huck and Tati stayed until Val finished the last cookie. They reminisced about working at Drip 'n' Donuts, about co-workers who had come and gone, about crazy things that happened during the graveyard shift, and they relived the glorious pay-it-forward streak that had bound them together forever. On the way out the door, Huck promised to mine her data and report back to Val with any pertinent sociological insights. Also, he thought to himself, he might find information relevant to his criminal investigation.

"If you want for me to hook you up with my cousin, just give me a call," Tati said to her just before Val closed the door.

"No, Tati. I'm sorry. You can't come with me."

Tati rolled her lower lip in a pouty face. "*¿Por qué?*"

Huck knew that she knew he had a weakness for the pouty face. Even so, she merely proved his point. "Because I'm going to the Booti Tooti Club."

She protested, "I can do Booti Tooti. I'm almost 20. I can go anywhere."

"Do you even know what the Booti Tooti Club is?"

"I've driven by. Looks like a dive." Tati stood straighter. "But so what? Really, I've been worse places. I had my first beer in the Sugar Shack. They're so sleazy they have a condom machine in the *women's* restroom."

"Do the women dance—"

"Of course, they dance! I danced when I went there."

"—naked?"

Tati had started to bust a dance move, and then the meaning of what Huck said clicked. "Oh." She stopped abruptly in the middle of a pirouette.

"The Booti Tooti Club glosses itself a 'gentleman's club,' but it's actually anything but. The waitresses are all nude and well oiled. In between serving overpriced, watered-down drinks to horny, desperate men, they perform contortions for their amusement on poles that are not so subtly intended to represent phalluses."

Huck refrained from mentioning the availability of even more salacious activities, such as lap dances, private performances, or rampant masturbation beneath tables and in individual booths. Even hearing his somewhat sanitized report, Tati seemed on the verge of vomiting.

Huck felt obliged to apologize. "I'm sorry to have to tell you about these kinds of places."

"Oh, I know all about titty bars. I don't care what sleazy dudes do to get their yayas off," she told him. "But I don't like *you* going there."

Huck agreed; he didn't like the idea of him going there, either. But that's where the trail of evidence led, so he had no choice. He promised, for his own sake as much as hers, to keep the visit as brief as possible, to focus on searching *only* for clues, and to remain standing—or at least cover the seat with a paper towel if he absolutely had to sit down.

Although Huck had never been to the Booti Tooti Club, he had heard, anecdotally, that another former co-worker from Drip 'n' Donuts worked there. Tank Turner, the erstwhile TurboChef oven operator at the donut shop, was employed at the club as a bouncer. All in all, that position suited him much better than toasting muffins. Huck liked Tank, for he empathized with the plight of all downtrodden blue-collar workers oppressed by capitalist society. At the same time, Huck chose his words carefully around Tank, because Tank openly despised anything he considered "weepy liberal bullshit." Tank's coarse demeanor changed little whether he was dead serious or just joking. He could say good morning and make it sound like a threat.

Pickups, four-wheel drive vehicles, late model muscle cars, lived-in vans, and sedans held together with duct tape filled the parking lot at the Booti Tooti Club. Huck parked his Prius across the street. The neon sign in the window blinked in sequence—Booti in red, Tooti in green, Club in blue, and finally Welcome in bright orange. Additionally, a red valentine heart ringed with shimmering white LED lights hung from the door, next to a sign that read, Valentine's Day Special—Inquire Within. Huck paused to wonder what manner of special bonuses were available upon inquiry, for those customers daring or foolish enough to ask.

Just inside the door, Huck felt himself sucked forward, as if into a negative pressure vortex created by so many gaping eyes all staring at the woman fingering herself on the stage. The stagnant air was heavy with sweat, flatulence, mouth breathing, spilled beer, residual smoke, and hormonal excretions. The rank amalgam of scents made Huck's eyes water. The light/dark contrast in the club was sharp, like a solid wall. The bar and the seating area were unlit, save for the occasional cigarette lighter struck by one of the customers to show appreciation for the performance. Darkness hid the spectators so that even men sitting side by side could barely see each other. The stage at the front of the room, though, was so bright it left afterimages on the inside of Huck's eyelids when he blinked.

Watching his steps carefully, Huck proceeded in the direction of the light. Front and center, the stage consisted of a raised concrete platform, through which a silver aluminum pole rose from floor to ceiling. At each corner of the stage was a spotlight mounted on a tripod and aimed at the pole, so the dome where their beams intersected was as bright as a sustained lightning flash. There, nude and glistening under the shocked white illumination, the main act—Nadine L'Amour, according to a poster behind the bar—hung upside down with her legs wrapped around the pole. She pulled herself higher, held on tight, threw back her head, and ground her pelvis into the pole, while purring, "*Yes, yes, ooooh yessss.*"

Huck studied the setting from a sociological perspective. Every time that Nadine stretched, squatted, or undulated, the men all turned their heads to readjust for optimal viewing. Naked and alone before the gaze of a phalanx of leering, lustful men with boners, she was utterly vulnerable. If they stormed the stage, not even Tank, who watched from a corner barstool, could have stopped the ensuing riot. Despite her exposure, though, Nadine taunted her clients. Being objectified seemed to empower her. While softly running her fingers across her skin, she looked briefly into each man's eyes, teasing him, daring him, yet leaving him wanting. By doing so, she turned her vulnerability into power, and their strength into unrequited lust. Her personal space was inviolable, no matter how urgently any one of them yearned to puncture it with their hands and other parts. So long as she was untouchable, she remained immune to shame or regret.

Nadine flashed a gander at Huck, and he lost his train of thought.

"Huck-o? Hey, kid. Well dip me in shit if that ain't really you." Tank Turner slapped Huck on the back hard enough to make him hiccup.

"You look good, Tank."

For Tank, "good" was relative to looking bitter, bothered, and bedraggled, which had been his normal disposition back when they worked at Drip 'n' Donuts. Clad in camouflage pants and a brown flannel shirt, he still looked bedraggled—but in a healthier way. Tank had always likened the Drip 'n' Donuts striped uniform shirt and baseball cap to an organ grinder monkey's costume, and, in protest, he wore it unwashed, wrinkled, buttoned incorrectly, and smelling like the bottom of a gym locker.

"I always knew sooner or later you'd show up here." He sidled closer to Huck and cackled into his ear, "That gal, Nadine, she's a fine piece of ass, ain't she?"

As a participant/observer doing field work, Huck knew he had to conform to local cultural mores to win the trust of his subjects. "Yes. She's a beautiful woman."

Tank elbowed Huck in the ribs. "That's what I'm talking about, kiddo. I always knew you weren't really gay, even if you didn't know it yourself."

"Human sexuality lies along a spectrum" he said.

"Not here," Tank asserted.

That, Huck agreed, was evident. One man seated by himself at a table up front whistled with two fingers and tossed a twenty dollar bill at Nadine's feet. She bent at the hips to retrieve it, butt high and thighs spread, and looked back at him from between her legs. This pose prompted a testosteronal deluge from the rest of the clientele, who hurled twenties at her from every corner of the room.

"Let me buy you a beer," Tank offered.

"Thanks," Huck said.

Tank walked to the cooler and pulled out two PBRs. He opened his and tilted it toward Huck, who recognized this gesture from beer commercials. Huck tapped the neck of his bottle against Tank's in a kind of toast. Huck said generically, "To good times."

"That's what you're here for, eh? Good times."

"Yes. Right. But I also want to ask you something."

"How would you like for Nadine to give you a private performance? I can fix you up with that."

"No. I mean, not right now." Huck fortified himself with a quick gulp of beer. "I was wondering, though. You've seen the news about Adam Erb, right?"

"Fucker got just what he deserved."

Huck's ears perked. "Why do you say that?"

"'Cause he's an ass-sucking warthog with a pencil dick and a mouth that spews diarrhea with every word he speaks."

"Other than that?"

"Motherfucker ripped me off."

"How so?"

As Tank spoke, his cheeks tensed and a vein on his temple throbbed. "Asshole used to come here sometimes. It was 'round about the time all them women accused him of harassment. I guess he couldn't get a date. Anyhow, he was particularly fond of one girl, Sybil Exxxotica. No surprise there. She was my biggest attraction—and I do mean *biggest*, as in K cup, get it?"

Huck cringed to think of such hideously deformed breasts.

Tank continued, "More than that, though, she was my lady."

"Do you mean your girlfriend?"

"No, Sybil was more than just a friend and definitely not a girl. She was my *lady*. We planned to get tattoos together."

"I'm sorry. What happened?"

"Adam fuckin' Erb happened!" Tank slammed his hand on the bar hard enough to rattle Huck's beer. "He came here exactly two years ago, on Valentine's Day. He waved a fistful of C-notes in her face. And she was gone, just like that. Never came back. Never said goodbye. But, stupid me, I still got my tattoo, and now I'm stuck with it." Tank pulled down the collar of his shirt to reveal the name Sybil inked above his heart.

"Did Adam Erb ever come back?"

"No. Good thing, too, 'cause if I ever saw him again, I'd have smashed his pretty little face into the pole. So that's why I say he got what he deserved." Tank slammed his fist on the bar counter.

As large and imposing a man as Tank was, Huck had never considered him capable of violence. He could usually get his way just by standing tall and squaring his shoulders. But when Tank spoke of Adam Erb, Huck noticed a growl in his voice rising from deep within, and when he struck the bar, it seemed to Huck like he vicariously punched Adam Erb in the nose.

"Gee. That's awful. I'm sorry that he stole your girl... your lady."

Tank finished the PBR, then burped loudly, as if letting go of the poison inside him. "Yeah, well, good riddance to Sybil. I don't miss that cunt. Now, I've got a good thing going with her...." Tank rolled his eyes toward Nadine, who winked back at him.

Huck watched Nadine bend over and wag her ass in front of a man's face. "It doesn't bother you? I mean, what she does?"

"Naw. Why should it? It's all just a show. She took over Sybil's special act, and she does it better."

"Her act?"

"Oh, yeah." Tank aimed his index finger in the air, as if pointing at an idea. "Would you like to watch, Huck-o? I guarantee you ain't never seen nothing like it."

Huck didn't see any graceful way out of this conundrum. He was curious about Ms. L'Amour's act, purely as a matter of investigative procedure. But deigning to patronize the sex industry was more than he could reconcile with his personal standards of behavior. So was his erection, but that was just an animal reaction.

Fortunately, having anticipated the possible need for a hasty exit, he'd come with just five dollars in his wallet, which he opened to show Tank.

"I'm a bit short on cash today," he said, hoping Tank would not offer this service on the house.

"Sorry," Tank apologized. "That ain't even enough to get you tickled by a feather. Rain check, then, kiddo."

"Yeah. Rain check."

CHAPTER 4

Two days after Adam Erb's murder, the drive-thru at Drip 'n' Donuts remained closed by police order. The donut shop was still open for walk-in business, but few entered. Outside, though, throngs of mourners built an impromptu shrine.

It began while police still processed the crime scene. Barb Knoop laid a mixed bouquet of plastic flowers she bought from the dollar store on the ground beneath the Thanks and Come Again sign at the exit of the drive-thru. Then she removed her Drip 'n' Donuts baseball cap, unfastened her name tag, ripped off her striped blouse, and left wearing just khaki trousers and a plus-size bra. Nobody had seen or heard from her since.

Soon thereafter, pilgrims contributed their own tokens to the memorial. They came alone or in groups; they left immediately or lingered; they cursed, lamented, stayed silent, consoled, eulogized, prayed, and demanded justice. They left myriad bouquets and ornate floral arrangements, crosses, candles, lanterns, glow sticks, balloons, beach balls, American flags, Confederate flags, MAGA caps, a Gideon Bible, panties and brassieres, human silhouette targets, a Brutus Buckeye bobblehead doll, a National Rifle Association tote bag, and an empty keg of PBR. The site also became a dumping ground for junk like an old lawnmower, a shovel with a broken handle, and dried up cans of paint. By the next morning, the drive-thru looked like a garage sale at a funeral home. And people kept coming.

Chavonne wanted nothing to do with it. For one thing, those people scared away customers. As a consequence, business was in the toilet. For another thing, they were nearly all white folks, who did not look especially friendly to her. This procession of bereaved Caucasians looked like the opposite of a pay-it-forward streak, because they looked more aggrieved than grieving.

So, when a black brother approached the Erb shrine, Chavonne took notice. He wore a brown leather jacket, dark glasses, and a porkpie hat. He stood in front of the shrine, shifting his weight from side to side, with his head down and arms dangling, like he was lost but didn't want to ask for directions. At length, with a satisfied grunt, he heaved a set of keys into the pile. "Shove it up your Erb," he shouted.

A pickup truck with an oversized American flag flapping in its bed pulled up behind him, and before its occupants could get out, the man escaped around the corner and slipped into the donut shop.

Once he was inside, Chavonne recognized him as the driver of the Erb-mobile. He shuffled by the front counter, past where Tati stood waiting to take his order, and skipped by several empty tables until he reached a corner booth. There, he slid in and sat with his head in his hands, looking out the window between his fingers and bouncing his feet heel to toe beneath the table. He seemed so antsy that Chavonne imagined he was breaking out in a rash right before her eyes. It was understandable — chauffeuring a murdered corpse around town would make anybody paranoid. The driver's nervous agitation reminded her that she'd awakened that morning with a headache, and remembering it brought it back.

"Can he just sit there like that?" Tati asked Chavonne. "Doesn't he have to order something?"

Indeed, as a deterrence against homeless persons, WiFi campers, and teenagers hanging out, store policy dictated that all on-site customers must make a minimum purchase of one item per hour. It was a dumb policy, because it granted sanctuary to anybody who could afford a dime for a donut hole every sixty minutes, but it came straight from the same corporate geniuses who practiced "leadership by kindness," yet complained about paying minimum wage. So what could you expect?

"I'll see what he wants," Chavonne said.

Jay-Rome was so fixated on staring out the window that he nearly jumped out of his shoes when Chavonne rapped on the table and asked, "Can I help yo'?"

"Hop off!" he cried out, then composed himself with a deep breath. He folded his arms and said, "I'm way sorry. It's just, well, what's going down with all them white peoples out there?"

"They're paying respects."

Jay-Rome sank into the booth. "Respect? He never gave none in life and don't deserve none just for being dead. I think they want some revenge."

"They do seem more pissed off than sad," Chavonne agreed. "I don't get it."

"Crackers stick together," Jay-Rome explained.

"So true." Chavonne offered a fist bump. "I'm Chavonne."

Jay-Rome bumped her back. "And I'm Jay-Rome."

"Can I get yo' a cup of coffee?" she asked. "It's on the house."

"Thanks, but no, I'm already jumpy."

"Last night I couldn't get myself to sleep, neither. So, I drank a cup of that green tea what's s'posed to calm a person down."

"Did it work?" Jay-Rome asked.

"No." Chavonne felt like her answer disappointed him.

Jay-Rome shrugged. "Can I have some, anyway? And maybe a devil's food donut?"

"That sounds copacetic," Chavonne replied, glad to do something helpful. She fetched him a cup of hot water, a teabag, and two devil's food donuts.

Jay-Rome lifted the teabag up and down by its string, as if he didn't know how it worked. "Sorry if I'm acting like all woo-woo," he said at length. "This whole situation is creeping me out. I can't shake these heebie-jeebies."

"Me neither," Chavonne empathized. "I ain't never seen a dead body before, let alone one that'd been tortured to death by sex. Now I can't get the image out of my brain."

"I hear you." He shook his head. "And, as if that ain't bad enough, people everywhere been givin' me the stink eye, like it's my fault he's dead. All I ever done was drive him around town wherever he wanted to go, without no word of thanks, too. It's not on me that he couldn't keep his willie in his pants."

"So true."

"What's worse of all is that now the po-lice call me a *person of interest*."

"Well, duh," Chavonne groaned. She pointed her index finger in the air, as if at some unseen authority figure. "They always blame the black person first."

"That's what I said to that lady cop, Detective Witt," Jay-Rome affirmed. "I went to the station to give a statement, and I told her, sure, I'll do whatever I can to help. When I got there, she took me into a room ain't no bigger than a closet and sat across from me at a steel table. She asked a million questions about every little thing I did that morning. Like, she asked what time I got up and what I ate for breakfast. What fuckin' difference does that make? She was more concerned about me eating an Egg McMuffin than about the garage being unlocked when I went to get the limo. Still, I did tell her everything I know. Then, like all at once, she got all up hot in my face and said that she knew I was a criminal. She asked, 'Where were you the night before Adam Erb was murdered?' and 'You hated Adam Erb, didn't you?' and 'Isn't it true you resented the way he treated you?' and finally, 'Didn't you wish that he was dead?'

"Last of all, she blurted out that they found my DNA all over the crime scene. No shit. I drive the damn limo."

Jay-Rome stood and opened his arms, as if pleading. Chavonne made a steadying, palms down gesture.

"That lady cop busted my balls like grapes. I thought she was going to arrest me. She said she was still watching me. Then, when that interrogation was all done, she smiled like my momma and wished me a good day."

Across the room, Tati, who'd been eavesdropping, called out, "¡Mierda!"

"Yeah so," Jay-Rome shouted back at her. "Whatever that means."

"Now I'm worried," Tati said. "Huck is on his way to meet with that detective, to give his statement. I should warn him."

"Tell him not to say nothing," Jay-Rome advised her. "Not even what he had for breakfast."

"That's the problem with Huck—" Chavonne started.

Tati finished her thought. "—he doesn't know how to stop talking."

As Detective Witt closed the door behind them, Huck heard a ping on his cell, and when he glanced at it, he saw an incoming text message from Tati. He left it to read later and silenced his phone, then stuffed it into his backpack.

The detective kept him waiting for almost an hour. Huck knew a common interrogation technique was to "ice" a subject by leaving them alone for a period of time to absorb the gravity of their circumstances and consider the consequences of the testimony they were about to give. He also presumed that she watched the whole time from behind the two-way mirror on the wall across from him. What didn't make sense to him, though, was why Detective Witt used those techniques on him. He came only to speak truth.

When she sat down across the table from him, the detective said, "Sorry to keep you waiting."

"No problem. I'm happy to tell you everything I know. I have some theories."

Detective Witt still hadn't looked directly at him. She opened a file and flipped through its contents as if seeing them for the first time; which, of course, Huck recognized as another technique, designed to make it appear she did not have an agenda.

"First, I need to confirm some background information," Detective Witt started. "Your proper name in Hyun-ki Carp—correct?"

"True that. But nobody has ever called me anything other than Huck. That was the deal my parents made with each other. My mother insisted on giving her firstborn child a Korean name, and my father agreed on the condition that I would go by my nickname, Huck. Personally, I like sharing that name with Huckleberry Finn, because I admire Mark Twain. Did you know he was a socialist and an atheist?"

"How did it happen that your mother, a South Korean woman, married a farmer from Danville, Ohio?"

"My father was a bachelor farmer in his forties. He found her name and photo in a catalog, then paid for her to come to America. Their marriage was purely transactional. But it worked. She learned English. Before he died, my father converted to Buddhism."

"Fascinating." Detective Witt twirled a pen in her hand, having not written down a word so far.

"It's not as unusual as you'd think. There are a lot of lonely farmers who will gladly convert to anything for a woman."

"But it must have been difficult for you growing up in a rural environment, where you stood out."

Huck dismissed her remark with a cursory tsk. He didn't want to be rude, but she was asking irrelevant questions, probably to establish a rapport with him. That's what they teach in the manual. Perhaps she didn't realize who she was dealing with.

"Do you know I'm a sociologist?" he asked.

"I do. So what?"

Huck placed both hands flat on the desk and leaned forward. "So, I have analyzed the clues of this crime."

Detective Witt dropped the pen; it bounced off the table and landed on the floor. Huck retrieved it for her, but she took another from behind her ear and pointed it at him.

"Let's start at the beginning," she suggested. "You were at the donut shop that morning because you were doing research, right?"

Finally, Huck thought. *It's about time she got to the point.*

"True that. I am studying reciprocal altruism between strangers."

"Paying it forward?"

"Exactly! Most sociobiologists believe that empathy evolved because cooperation is essential to hunter-gatherer cultures. People do favors for others because they expect to receive favors in return. Quid pro quo is an innate construct, not a social one. Adam Erb was an exception. He didn't have an altruistic bone in his body."

"Uh huh. So, you knew Adam Erb?"

Huck noticed Detective Witt glance at the two-way mirror, as if confirming something to whomever watched on the other side.

"Yes. Well, not personally. Adam Erb was trapped in his own cult of personality. He didn't exist without the affirmation of his followers. In his world, if he couldn't take credit for something, it didn't happen. That's why he refused to pay it forward."

"Ouch." Detective Witt bit her lower lip and shook her head disdainfully. "It sounds like he contradicted your pet theory. That must've aggravated you."

Huck felt like he was teaching Sociology 101 to the freshman class. "Adam Erb is just another variable I need to take into consideration. All good research has to account for outliers."

Detective Witt winced, then cleared her throat. "Tell me what you saw when you found the body."

"Judging from the condition of the body, I'd estimate he'd been dead six to twelve hours. I know he uploaded his latest podcast at 10:00 p.m., so he was at his home studio at that time. He remained online checking various Internet sites until 10:15 p.m. I therefore surmise that he was murdered in his own house and taken to the limo. My guess is that there were no signs of a break-in, so he must have known the perpetrator and let that person in. I imagine he had a security camera, but I'd also guess it was wiped clean. Am I right?"

"Those are interesting assumptions." Detective Witt said, neither confirming nor refuting Huck's assertion; however, she began taking notes, so he felt encouraged to continue.

"I saw no defensive wounds on the body. I believe, then, that the victim initially agreed to what happened, even allowing himself to be handcuffed. Thus, when things went awry, he was bound and incapable of fighting back. He was also probably drunk.

"As to the cause of death, I had a friend in my department's lab analyze the little blue pills in the candy hearts and confirm they were high-dosage sildenafil, aka Viagra. Maybe the victim ate a few of these of his own volition, unsuspecting. However, once he was restrained, the perpetrator continued feeding him erectile dysfunction medication. Most likely, at some point Adam tried to resist, but the perpetrator forced more of the Viagra-infused candy into his mouth, then covered it with a hand, so he had no choice but to swallow. Eventually, this resulted in an overdose, which accounts for the body's, uh, tumescence, and most likely caused a heart attack."

"The coroner has not completed her autopsy," Detective Witt informed Huck. "We don't know yet. Your speculation is interesting, though. What else did you notice?"

"The perpetrator staged Adam's body to make a statement. He was masked, suggesting that he hid his true self. He wore a bow tie and held a yellow rose, as in his photo on the cover of *Columbus Monthly*, when they named him Ohio's most eligible bachelor. The perpetrator was mocking his popularity and his playboy persona.

"Soon after Adam became Ohio's most eligible bachelor, women started coming out with accusations of sexual harassment against him, and his popularity tanked. He went from being a celebrated socialite to a social pariah in a matter of days. Afterwards, he disappeared from public view for several months. However, I've learned that during this time he frequented a strip club called the Booti Tooti Club."

"I know that place," Detective Witt said.

Huck continued without acknowledging her. "As if to emasculate him, the perpetrator placed Adam in a subordinate sexual position with a blow-up doll and dressed him in a chastity belt. Apropos of that, I noticed that the chastity belt was identical to that of the logo of the so-called Society of Enlightened Celibate Savants."

"What's a savant?" the detective queried.

Huck paused to wonder if playing dumb was also some kind of interrogation technique? No matter, he didn't want to interrupt his train of thought.

"Items found with the body suggest that the perpetrator knew Adam's to do list for the following day. The skull ring was from the logo of the Buckeye

State Babes Motorcycle Club, and the helmet was like that worn by the Milk Maids roller derby team—he was scheduled to meet with both groups the next morning. The squirt gun, the beer, and the cowboy boots all represent other locations where he was appearing that day. Finally, the perpetrator wrote #pERBvert on the victim's chest, which soon became a social media trend. My conclusion is that the perpetrator intended to ridicule not only Adam Erb, but also his fans and followers, both the former ones who turned on him and the current ones who embraced him. Adam Erb was a reputation chameleon, loved by those who hate him and hated by those who love him, just at different times.

"But here's another intriguing clue. The cowboy boots he wore likely refer to his appearance Friday evening at Daisy Mae's Moonshiner Tavern. But that was a late addition to his schedule, which he hadn't yet posted on his web page."

Detective Witt wagged a finger at Huck. "How did you obtain all of this information?"

"You can't hide from the Internet," Huck said.

The detective scoffed.

Again, Huck felt like he had to speak down to her. "Are you aware of the sensation that this murder has created on social media? This morning, the hottest trend in Columbus was #KillERB. There are a million ideas, opinions, and theories, and each of those spins off a million comments. The Erb brand is even bigger now than when he was alive. It's the murder that launched a million memes."

"The fucking Internet is the best thing that ever happened to criminals," Detective Witt remarked.

"And sociologists," Huck added.

"Okay then. But what about the cigar?" she asked.

Huck shrugged. "I'm not sure about that one."

"Well, one thing is for sure—a cigar is never just a cigar." Detective Witt grinned, apparently pleased at having trumped Huck.

But Huck was already thinking ahead. He scratched his head and closed his eyes to concentrate. "One thing I can't figure out is why the murderer wanted for the body to be discovered in the donut shop drive-thru."

"Maybe it had something to do with your research?" Detective Witt speculated. "Maybe it was because he broke your pay-it-forward streaks, going all the way back to that famous one five years ago that nearly broke a record. Is it possible that the body was meant for you, personally, to discover?"

Of course he had considered that possibility, but Huck deliberately withheld mentioning it. It unnerved him that the detective had come up with that idea on her own. Perhaps she was craftier than he gave her credit for.

Detective Witt's chair screeched against the hard floor as she suddenly stood up and scowled at Huck. She articulated each syllable when she asked, "Now, professor, do you want to hear what I think?"

"Uh, of course. I'm happy to collaborate."

"You're a regular Sherlock Holmes, ain't you?"

"Well, I *am* a sociologist," Huck beamed. "It's like being a detective."

"Bullshit!" Detective Witt grimaced and waved her badge in front of Huck's face. "You have to have one of these to be a detective."

"I meant no disrespect."

"Sure. And I mean no disrespect when I say you don't know what the fuck you're talking about."

That stung, but Huck thought it prudent not to correct her on that fallacious assumption. Instead, he propped his head on the back of his fist, ready to listen.

"Here are five things I know for sure." Detective Witt counted on her hand, raising another finger for each point she made. "One: you took it upon yourself to 'examine' the crime scene before the police arrived. Two: in doing so, you tampered with evidence. Three: you know a suspicious amount of detail about the murder. Four: you disliked Adam Erb to begin with. And...."

Detective Witt threw down the file onto the desk. Huck noticed his name on its tab. She clenched her jaws and sneered the final point through her teeth. "Five: you do not have an alibi for the night of the murder."

Huck felt each one of the detective's points like a slap to the face. To the last point, he objected, "You don't know that!"

"Then tell me, what were you doing on Friday night from 10:00 p.m. until Saturday morning at 6:00 a.m?"

"Uh, sleeping," he replied sheepishly.

"Alone?"

"Yes, alone."

Detective Witt turned her back to Huck and faced the two-way mirror. Her ponytail was rubber banded so tight that he could see the knob of her axis vertebrae. Her shoulder blades were so tense he could see their outline beneath her plaid shirt. She spoke while looking back at Huck in the mirror.

"That will be all for now, Mr. Carp."

"I'm only trying to help."

When she did not reply, Huck rose slowly, careful to lift the chair instead of pushing it so it wouldn't screech. He backed out the door on the balls of his feet. Detective Witt pulled the door shut behind him.

Huck felt a panic attack coming on. While rummaging through his backpack for his bottle of Valium, he found his cell and remembered the text message from Tati. He opened it and read, *G-Luck 2U. B careful, tho. JR sez Witt EVIL.*

Huck groaned, wondering how the interview might have gone if he'd read the text beforehand. It hadn't occurred to him that the detective would be anything other than collegial and appreciative of his expertise. On second thought, though, he supposed that niceness was not a particularly useful quality in a detective from the Special Victims Bureau. Now, he felt not so much threatened as disappointed. He really wanted to be part of this investigation. If he was going to solve this crime, he'd have to do it on his own.

A large corkboard hung on the far wall of the detective's office—Detective Witt called it her "crazy board," because by the time she was done with any case, there would be so many Post-it notes, cards, photos, newspaper clippings, and assorted cut and pastings on it connected by lines of yarn tacked from one to the other to another that it looked like the product of a disturbed mind. Sometimes it was more confusing than useful, but creating one was standard investigative procedure for a detective, so she took her crazy board dead serious. Not even the slightest, most insignificant clue went unpinned. If nothing else, it made it look like she was working hard. Whether it ever helped her solve a crime, she couldn't exactly say.

Detective Will had kept her file on Adam Erb from when she had investigated charges of sexual misconduct. Unfortunately, those cases were dropped. Now, however, everything she had learned about Adam Erb was relevant again. There was an abundance of clues, suspects, and possible motives for murdering him. She had halfway expected that one day Adam Erb would meet with foul play. Death by Viagra, however, she had not envisioned. Bludgeoning by a giant dildo, asphyxiation in a head-sized condom, and drowning in spermicide *had* occurred to her. If working so long in SVB had taught her anything, it was that sex, death, and revenge often went hand in hand.

Already, the crazy board was a crowded patchwork, with a spider's web of yarn lines connecting everything to everything else. There was plenty of room for one more item, though. Detective Witt took a photo of Huck from the file folder with his name on it. She moved a photo of Jay-Rome to the side and stapled Huck's in its place, directly beneath a picture of Adam Erb's body taken at the crime scene. She then tacked a line of yarn between them.

Running her eyes back and forth over these materials, Detective Witt grumbled "Hmm" and chortled "Uh huh," and then she snapped her fingers and said aloud, "A ha." She dialed her captain's extension, and when he picked up, she said, "Good morning, captain. I need to get a search warrant."

CHAPTER 5

Val Vargas hadn't slept in three days. It felt like her body was plugged into a supercomputer's USB port that kept her constantly overcharged. Data streams exploded across her monitors so fast that watching them made her brain feel like neural spaghetti. If she closed her eyes, she saw scrolling afterimages of code flash across the dark insides of her eyelids. It almost hurt.

Val had never felt more alive.

In the last forty-eight hours, social media traffic throughout the greater Columbus metropolitan area had broken so many records she could barely keep up—most views, most postings, most shares, most comments, most shoutouts, most likes, most dislikes, most pokes, and, for Val personally, most new follower requests in a twenty-four hour period. At one point, #LongLivERB and #DeathToERB replaced each other as the most liked and most disliked hashtags. This mania for all things Erb transcended diverse apps, sites, media, and platforms; it didn't matter whether the source was postings on Twitter, homemade videos on YouTube, or any of the countless Instagram and Pinterest photos, new ceilings for social media activity were being set, in real time, and Val alone bore witness to its entirety.

Early on Valentine's Day morning, all top-ten locally-trending hashtags were Erb-related. From amid the social media clamor, though, four major players emerged as leading trendsetters.

Two of them were anonymous. They went by the aliases @LadyMuleskinner and @MadameSECSY.

@LadyMuleskinner was a relative social media newcomer, whose output proliferated in the aftermath of Adam Erb's murder. Her hashtags evoked a cowboy motif, such as #GunslingERB, #WranglERB, and #SixShootERB. In them, she cast Adam in various roles from old Western movies. Sometimes he was a mustache-twirling villain; other times he wore the white hat of a hero. Fans and haters alike interpreted her posts to confirm their preferred biases. Her most popular hashtag was #PutERBtoBedWet, as in, *Poor Adam was rode hard and #PutERBtoBedWet.*

What did it mean? Was she grieving or gloating? Many citizens presumed it meant something sexual, which supported several of the more licentious theories about the cause of his death. Some speculated that he died as the result of a forgotten safe word, a bizarre fetish gone wrong, a failed masturbatory experiment, a gang rape from aggrieved lovers, or a botched sex-reassignment surgery. Only @LadyMuleskinner knew for sure what she meant.

By contrast, @MadameSECSY was already a familiar person in the local Twitterverse. As the founding mother of the Society of Enlightened Celibate Savants, she was well known, although nobody knew her true identity. In the aftermath of Adam Erb's murder, the mysterious madame proffered an ongoing series of cryptic aphorisms under the #ProvERBs hashtag, such as:

#ProvERB1. "Safe Sex" is an oxymoron.

#ProvERB2. Nothing in life is more real than fantasies.

#ProvERB3. The same region of the brain that controls lies, controls sex.

#ProvERB4. Consent in the evening doesn't prevent regret in the morning.

#ProvERB5. There's what he said, what she said, and then there's truth nobody said.

By Sunday morning, @MadameSECSY was up to #ProvERB62. These pithy maxims were viewed by hundreds of thousands, inspired copious likes and comments, and were shared or retweeted so many times that tracking them was like mapping the ripples in a pond during a hailstorm. Meanwhile, applications for membership in SECS snowballed with every new posting. From a marketing standpoint, @MadameSECSY had found the holy grail.

Additionally, two of the most-viewed online sensations were created by local media personalities. They were locked in a virtual cat fight for the city's attention.

@GinnyCampbell scored numerous likes and shares with her self-made video, "Eulogy for Adam Erb." She posted her Erb-opic on the WXOF News Squadron homepage. The epitaph featured clips of stories about and interviews with Adam Erb that Ginny had done over the years. They told the story of Adam's rise as a purveyor of ladies' intimate apparel to his fabulous success designing what came to be called "Columbus chic" fashions. The tribute showed footage of Adam appearing at local events like the Jazz and Ribs Fest where he took the first ceremonial bite, the Doo Dah parade where he was grand marshal, and Monster Truck Jam Columbus where he waved the checkered flag. Ginny's obituary glossed over the period of Adam's troubles by merely alluding to "unsubstantiated accusations that were later dropped." Finally, she concluded with the evening magazine segment of her and Adam together in the studio of his popular *Talking Truth* podcast. Ginny bore witness to when Adam first uttered what became his signature sign-off: "The truth ain't right or wrong—it's just true."

Meanwhile, not to be outdone, @DGlint! broadcast her own hastily assembled Erb montage, entitled, "The Checkered Legacy of Adam Erb." In addition to boilerplate material from the prewritten obituary the station had on file, D'Nisha added footage from her interview with one of Erb's former employees, who accused him of making unwanted sexual overtures toward her. In D'Nisha's opinion, the moment when she asked, "What would you like to say to Adam Erb?" and the woman broke down, sobbing, "Why, Adam, oh *why*?" represented the nadir of Erb's fall from grace. At the end of the feature, D'Nisha stood in front of a plain white background, looked straight into the camera, and said, "Adam Erb was an enigma. He was famous, but few people actually *knew* him. Perhaps Adam Erb did not even know himself."

That last line triggered a new hashtag, #StrangERB. Within an hour, it blasted to the top of the trends list like a rocket fueled with indignant estrogen.

This was the kind of stuff Val lived for. As the sun rose over Columbus on Valentine's Day morning, Val gulped a couple Adderall with Red Bull and braced herself for another day of high drama on the social media frontier. She couldn't wait to see what kinds of blogged tantrums, clickbait scandals, cyber mysteries, and virtual conspiracy theories the day would bring. Best of all, she alone would observe the entire Erb online phenomenon as it unfolded, and record it for posterity. Val owned this little piece of Internet history.

When Ginny Campbell learned Adam's fans were going to gather to celebrate his life in the drive-thru at Drip 'n' Donuts, she liked the idea so much that she took it over. She amplified the message through social media and implied she was hosting the event. No one else was taking credit for it, so she might as well.

It was a win-win situation, because her presence would attract a larger audience, with the additional benefit of giving her a major ratings victory, too. Adam would've approved of her exploiting his death for fame and profit.

Ha! Ginny thought. *That slut D'Nisha Glint will go ballistic with envy.*

At noon on Valentine's Day, the crowd around Drip 'n' Donuts spilled from the drive-thru, into the parking lot, and onto the sidewalk on Cleveland Avenue. A long queue of pilgrims waited for a chance to visit and add their own tokens to the growing Erb memorial. Many people waved American flags. Many others carried homemade cardboard signs with You Can't Kill the Truth written in magic marker. Some women wept. Some men wore camouflage and carried not-so-concealed firearms. Somebody in the throng shouted "Erb lives," which turned into a chant.

At the front of the assembly, Ginny surveyed the proceedings while waiting for Troll to set up for broadcast. Adam Erb 's shrine had grown so massive that its shadow completely covered the Drip 'n' Donuts drive-thru. More and more odd items had accumulated in the heap, such as wind chimes, pink flamingos, cheerleader pom-poms, homemade apple pies, a clothier's inventory worth of discarded female undergarments, confetti made from the *Columbus Dispatch*, and over a hundred heart-shaped boxes of Valentine's Day candy. For some reason, somebody had left a stack of romance novels beneath the drive-thru window. Ginny picked up one entitled *Stranger in Town* and flipped through its pages. From start to finish, the hero's name had been crossed out and replaced with "Adam."

Ginny couldn't decide if that was touching, delusional, or just plain weird. Gazing into the crowd, she wondered who among them had done that, and she realized it could have been anyone. Maybe even one of those bearded, tobacco-chewing men had a private appetite for romance novels.

When Troll flashed a thumbs up, Ginny rubbed her eyes to produce tears, then hopped onto a makeshift stage of stacked forklift pallets. "Welcome," she said into her microphone. Once the crowd simmered down, she opened her arms and let the breeze toss her hair. Ginny wore a little black silk taffeta dress with lace sleeves and a V-neck, a mesh chiffon cape over her shoulders, and a pillbox hat with tulle veil that covered the top of her brow. Her wardrobe did little to protect her against the cold, but evoked just the right blend of sexuality and mourning. She gave them a moment to soak in her ambiance, while blinking to release the tears. Weeping was a good look for her.

"Adam would've been humbled to see so many fans gathered here today. He touched us. He cared for us. He spoke to us. He said the things we wished we could say. Let us never forget his words!"

Sobs and applause followed.

"Adam was born of modest means in a proud working-class neighborhood. Although he rose to great heights of success, he never forgot where he came from. He was truly one of us."

Wails and cheers rang out. Ginny steeled her features against the compulsion to smile. *They're eating this up.*

"Adam was a wealthy man, not only in material riches, but also in spiritual resolve. Sure, like every man, he had flaws, but he refused to let them define him. His enemies misunderstood him; some would say they persecuted him. Through it all, though, Adam spoke truth to us, even when it was hard to hear. That's what a friend does. And Adam Erb was my friend."

She held the microphone above her head to catch the roar of the crowd when she declared, "And Adam Erb was your friend too!"

She nodded to Troll, who blew her a kiss back — *huh?* — before turning his camera to pan the faces in the crowd. People's mouths gaped and their eyes burned; they stomped their feet and waved their arms over their heads. Ginny felt like a general giving a pep talk to troops prior to battle. She stood with chin raised and arms folded. *I'm freakin' Joan of Arc,* she thought.

Ginny continued, "Each of us will remember Adam in our own way. But I've invited one special person to share her thoughts and feelings with us."

Ginny wiggled her finger for Barb Knoop, who was blowing her nose behind the WXOF van, to come forward. Barb was trembling, her hair a mess. Dressed in a faded leather jacket, she breathed in the cold air hard enough to raise great clouds of steam. Ginny thought she looked like pure trailer trash, which was *perfect*.

When Barb stepped onto the platform, Ginny put one arm over her shoulder and held the microphone in front of her with the other. "I'm so glad you're here. Can you tell us your name?"

"My name is Barb," the woman said.

"You work here, right?"

"*Worked* here. I done quit."

"Very well, you worked here. Tell me what you want to share about Adam Erb."

She chewed gum. "I cain't say I knew Adam Erb well. But I was a big fan. I met him once, at Daisy Mae's Moonshiner Tavern. He asked me to do the sweetheart dance with him. He was real kind to me."

"But there's more to your story, isn't there, Barb?" Ginny asked.

Barb puffed her cheeks and exhaled. "Well, I'll just say that after our dance, one thing led to another...."

Come on, Ginny thought. *Spill it out.*

"We had a special night together. He gave me much more than just a memory."

"How so?"

"I'm knocked up with Adam Erb's baby."

D'Nisha Glint had saved her secret for just the right moment. First, Adam Erb was murdered, and suddenly everybody was talking about him. She briefly considered the decorum of going public now; to some, it might seem belated, or even disrespectful. However, D'Nisha gambled she held the moral high ground, and, even if not, nothing captured ratings like a good scandal. Second, any lingering doubts disappeared when that skank ass-kissing Ginny Campbell organized a memorial ceremony for Adam. She couldn't just sit back, do nothing, and let Ginny scoop her.

Besides, if anybody had a right to rake Adam Erb's name through the mud for personal gain, she did.

D'Nisha had a juicy story of her own to tell. She decided to answer Ginny's blatant ratings grab by tweeting to her followers that she had a confession to make, which she would livestream prime time on Valentine's Day. Instead of using the WCBN studio, she delivered her testimony at home, in front of her bookcase, which she'd filled with classics of literature and philosophy she'd never read. She took down the dogs playing poker poster on the wall and replaced it with an original print of the Columbus skyline. She'd never gone on air without wearing her contacts, but for this occasion she chose a pair of glasses with rectangular red frames—she didn't want to look too beautiful, lest her audience not relate to her. Finally, she placed her laptop open on the desk facing of her, centered herself for the camera, and clicked to begin.

"Happy Valentine's Day, friends." D'Nisha said. "Today is for love, candy, hugs and kisses—and I wish all of the above for all of you. You're the best fans in the whole world."

She bowed her head.

"But, for me, this day also brings back some painful memories. I've kept them inside for years. I can't any longer. Please be advised that the following may disturb some viewers."

D'Nisha leaned forward as if to whisper a secret in somebody's ear.

"Okay. Are you still with me?" She pressed her hands together, as if in prayer. "I need to unburden myself. This story is about the late Adam Erb. It's horrible how he died. Nobody deserves that. But he was not blameless. I know that, personally."

She dabbed her eyes with a tissue.

"I met Adam Erb when I was twenty-one years old. I had just been crowned Butter Queen of the Ohio State Fair. He approached me at the horseshoeing exhibit. Of course, I knew who he was. Adam Erb! The fashion mogul! The socialite! The celebrity! For goodness' sake, he'd just been voted the most eligible bachelor in Columbus. My heart was in my throat when he introduced himself. I felt like one of those famous butter sculptures, melting.

"He congratulated me and asked if I'd ever done any modeling. Well, before I became a serious journalist, I dreamt of becoming a top model, so I was absolutely beside myself when he explained he wanted a 'fresh look' for his new line of Savage Desires lingerie. He said I might be the woman he was looking for. I couldn't agree fast enough to do a photo shoot. Little did I know what he *really* had in mind."

She looked away as if pained, then returned her gaze unblinking into the camera.

"I was in my dressing room. I was wearing a red bow tie teddy when Adam just let himself in, without even knocking. He said he wanted to see the *merchandise*, so I posed for him. He said I seemed nervous. Well, truthfully, I was. When he said he knew how to calm my nerves, I thought he meant yoga or meditation, or something like that. But he came closer to me. And—"

She hardened her cheeks. "That's when he put his hands on me."

D'Nisha allowed that statement to register for a second before proceeding.

"I never spoke about this before. At first, I kept quiet because I was afraid to risk my modeling career. The ad campaign—'The girl next door has Savage Desires'—was a big hit. Soon thereafter, I got a job as the weatherwoman at WCBN, and later as a reporter. I tried to put that whole incident with Adam behind me. Much later, when brave women began coming forward with accusations of sexual harassment, I kept my secret still. I told myself that in order to maintain journalistic objectivity, I could not do otherwise.

"But now, Adam Erb is gone. And that's sad. But recently another member of the media eulogized him like a hero. That was the last straw! I can remain silent no longer!"

She clenched a fist and shook it in front of her. "Adam Erb assaulted me too."

CHAPTER 6

Tati was upset that Ximena didn't ask if she had anything special planned for Valentine's Day, like she did every year. Usually, that question pissed her off. First, her personal life was none of her mother's damn business. Second, the answer was most often no. She'd made no special plans, nobody gave her candy or would take her out to a romantic dinner, and she sure as hell wasn't going to get any of the kind of action that Valentine's Day was invented for.

This year, though, Tati had a better answer.

But her mother never asked. This was unacceptable, because she needed her mother to talk her into doing what she wanted to do. Without a nudge, she didn't know if she had the courage to ask Huck on a date.

It was just like her mother to butt into her affairs when she didn't want her to, but to give her space when she desperately needed some good advice. How did she always seem to know what *not* to do?

At the breakfast table, Tati couldn't take it any longer. She waited until her mother had poured herself a cup of coffee and sat down, and then she pulled up a chair across from her. "Today is Valentine's Day."

"So it is, *mija*," Ximena said. "I am going to bake red velvet cupcakes shaped like a heart. *¿Te gusta?*"

"*¡Mama!*" Tati threw her hands in the air. "Are you trying to make me fat?"

Ximena lurched back in her seat, as if she'd just gotten an electric shock.

"My bad," Tati apologized, feeling guilty. "But I gained two pounds this week. I eat too many donuts at work. So, no cupcakes for me."

"Two pounds? *Es nada.* I've seen mangoes that weigh more." Ximena sipped her coffee, then held the cup in both hands. "But why don't you tell me what is really bothering you."

"I am..." Now that her mother had invited her to spill the beans, she didn't know what to say. "...*frustrated*, that's what I am."

"*¿Por que?*"

"I don't want to stay home with you doing nothing on Valentine's Day. I want to go out with a *man*." She sucked in a breath. "I want *Huck* to take me out."

"Huck?"

"*Si*, Huck."

"*¡Dios mío!*" Ximena made a sign of the cross. "Finally. For so long, I have wanted for you and Huck to — *¿Cómo se dice?* — 'hook up.'"

Tati was glad to hear it. But she wished her mother had said it sooner. Or, said it to Huck for her.

"I like him. But I think he sees me like a little sister. When you worked with him at Drip 'n' Donuts, he thought of you as a mother. Really, he did. You sewed his buttons. You kept an extra pair of socks for him to wear when he came to work with them mismatched."

"Huck was absentminded. He needed help remembering things."

"I could do that for him," Tati declared. "And more, too. But although I try to get him to look at me, he doesn't notice."

Ximena put down her coffee cup and reached across the table for Tati's hand. "There are many things that Huck doesn't notice. He is brilliant, *si*, but he does not know himself. And he truly does not know women. Did you know that he once had a little girlfriend?"

"*Si*. I knew."

"And before that he had a boyfriend."

Tati winced. "*Si, si, si*. I knew that too. That doesn't bother me. He was just experimenting."

"But did you know that his girlfriend was his boyfriend's sister?"

"No. That's kind of messed up. But I don't think that matters."

"You're right. It doesn't. I tell you not to be discouraging. No. I want you to understand. Huck lives in his thoughts. But he hasn't yet discovered his heart."

"So true. Sometimes I see him staring into his computer with those deep brown eyes of his, studying words and numbers that I don't understand." She grunted and scrunched her cheeks. "And it just drives me so *loco* that I just want to grab him where it matters and say — hey, professor, analyze this."

In the ensuing moment of silence, Tati realized what she had just divulged to her mother. She expected Ximena to shoo her away from the table and demand that she go to Mass immediately. Instead, Ximena exhaled a chuckle and said, "It's worth a try."

Huck couldn't get to his computer because it was stowed in Chavonne's office, and she had barricaded herself inside. When she had reported for work that afternoon, she announced that she did not want to be disturbed and slammed the door so hard it shook the donut trays behind the counter. This was an unprecedented violation of her open door policy, which led staff to speculate that she was depressed and angry because it was Valentine's Day and she didn't have a boyfriend. Under most circumstances, Huck admired Chavonne's poise under pressure. The trials of managing Drip 'n' Donuts were considerable, from dealing with perpetual staff shortages, to placating irate customers, to complying with the idiots at corporate headquarters. Not even a drive-thru murder fazed her.

A broken heart, though, sent her into hiding. Some people just weren't constitutionally capable of dealing with the stress, woes, and turmoil that came with love. For them, celibacy was perhaps the healthiest choice.

Huck stuck around the donut shop in hope that Chavonne would come out and he could gain access to his computer. His coffee had gone cold, though, and he'd just decided to leave and look for something more productive to do, when Tati entered the shop. Huck thought it peculiar since she wasn't scheduled to work.

A customer sitting at the counter whistled at her flirtatiously.

Huck did a double take. He'd never seen her not wearing her Drip 'n' Donuts uniform. Indeed, beneath her denim jacket she wore a red cashmere dress with a ruffled hem several inches above her knees, and mid-calf black leather high-heeled boots. *She must be freezing*, he thought.

Her hair was done in corkscrew curls. She wore smokey mascara and ruby red lipstick.

"Tati," was as much as he could get out while still processing everything different about her.

"Hi, Huck. Were you leaving?"

The question helped him focus. "Yes. I can't get any work done. My computer is in Chavonne's office, and she's closed the door."

"Is something wrong with her?"

"I'm guessing it has something to do with Valentine's Day."

Tati stepped closer to Huck, positioning herself between him and the exit. He caught a scent that might have been lily of the valley.

She made eye contact, bit her lip, and then spoke. "I wanted to say, that is, I wanted to ask, if you don't have anything special or important to do, I thought, maybe, we could get dinner, or maybe drinks, together. What do you say?"

Huck could not reason through all the variables to formulate an immediate answer. What were Tati's intentions? Possibly, she meant her overture collegially — it was dinnertime, after all. They had to eat, right? However, Tati's appearance, comportment, and overall demeanor were uncharacteristically risqué, especially in the context of Valentine's Day. This reinforced a suspicion that she was making a romantic proposition to him. Her signals short-circuited his mental faculties, leaving him without a working theory of what to do next.

While he compiled the data and weighed his response, the sound of police sirens on Cleveland Avenue distracted Huck.

Tati put her hand on top of his. "Well, Huck? What do you say?"

"I think that—"

Before he could finish his sentence, three police cruisers peeled into the Drip 'n' Donuts parking lot and screeched to a stop in front of the entrance. Detective Sally Witt scrambled out of the lead car before it had come to a complete stop. "Columbus Police, Special Victims Bureau," she declared and showed her badge as she kicked in the door.

Chavonne rushed out of the office. "What's all this fuss and bother?"

Detective Witt strutted straight to Huck. She removed handcuffs from a loop on her belt and slapped them onto Huck's wrists, while he stood frozen in shock and disbelief.

Tati poked the detective in the chest. "You can't do that to Huck."

Detective Witt pushed Tati aside with a forearm, then pointed a finger at Huck, inches from his nose. She seemed to savor each word when she said, "Hyun-ki Carp, you are under arrest for the murder of Adam Erb."

CHAPTER 7

Tati was angry, anxious, scared, and generally freaked out about visiting Huck in the Franklin County Corrections Center. The building was a gray square, and it cast a cold shadow over her. At the bottom of the stairs, a gauntlet of unpleasant-looking people paced back and forth on the sidewalk, holding signs that read Justice for Adam Erb, An Eye for an Erb, and You Can't Kill the Truth.

This is for Huck, she told herself as she hurried past them.

Once inside the lobby, Tati felt relieved to have made it past the mob, but then it hit her that she was now in jail — aka, the clink, the slammer, the big house. No matter what she called it, this was a dangerous place to enter. She had an unpaid and long overdue parking ticket that, if discovered, she worried would give the cops a reason to lock her up, too. She'd heard stories about Hispanic friends and family being detained for less, like Uncle Mateo's best friend's neighbor who got pulled over for a burned-out taillight, and the next thing he knew was on a plane bound for Tapachula.

A uniformed cop barked at her to move along. When going through the metal detector, she set off an alarm and instinctively raised her arms over her head as if surrendering. She'd emptied her pockets and removed all jewelry, so the only thing that might have triggered the alarm was her underwire bra, and that was not something she felt inclined to confide, not even to the only female officer on duty. Instead, she submitted to a pat down, and was relieved when the cop let her proceed without requiring a body-cavity search.

Tati reminded herself that seeing Huck was worth this ordeal. It distressed her to think of him at the mercy of such a strictly regimented system. She came prepared, having completed all required documentation in advance. When queried about her relationship with the inmate, she'd mulled her response, thinking that "friend" was insufficiently intimate to grant her admission. She wrote "girlfriend" in the blank space, but then erased it and modified her answer to "fiancée." She hoped Huck wouldn't find out.

Tati sat in the waiting room, thinking about that awful day when the cops came for Huck. Watching him get arrested right in front of her eyes, on Valentine's Day no less, was a nightmare come true. Worst of all, before the cops burst in, he was on the brink of agreeing to a date. The next thing she knew, instead of having dinner with her in a candlelit booth, a scowling Detective Witt was putting Huck in handcuffs while reading him his rights. Tati had wrapped her arms over Huck's shoulders and cried out with all her heart, "No, no, no, no, no. You can't. *He's mine!*"

"No. He's ours," the detective replied and pulled her away from Huck.

"It's okay," Huck said to her. "This is all a misunderstanding."

The detective snorted; it sounded like she scraped snot and phlegm from halfway down her esophagus. Tati thought she was going to spit a loogie on her.

Meanwhile, Chavonne had recorded the entire incident on her phone. "Watch yo'self," she called to Detective Witt. "I'm putting this movie up on that Instagram."

"C'mon, perv," Detective Witt sneered at Huck, pulling him up by his collar. "We're going to have a nice old-fashioned interrogation."

"I want a polygraph," Huck said. "I have nothing to hide."

"I'll let you know when I've heard the truth." She pushed Huck toward the door; he dragged his heels.

Tati shuddered as she watched the detective push down on Huck's head to load him into the back of the police cruiser. He looked shocked, as if until that moment he disbelieved what was happening. Huck gazed back at her from the rear window as the vehicle pulled away. Tati jogged behind, shouting "I won't forget you," and hoping that Huck could hear.

Now she sat in the waiting room at the Franklin County Corrections Center, with her head throbbing like she was nursing a hangover. The women waiting with her — they were all women — seemed like they knew the drill. They watched the clock. They checked their makeup. Some of them knew each other and inquired about jobs, kids, families, lawyers, court dates, and other pertinent topics. Unlike her, none of them seemed any more apprehensive about being there than they would about waiting for their number to be called at a delicatessen.

I don't belong here, Tati thought. *And neither does Huck.*

When the guard called her name, Tati shivered, realizing, for the first time, that she had no idea what she would say to Huck. She'd invested so much thought and energy into just getting there that she'd failed to anticipate what to do next. The guard led her down a long hallway with cinder block walls and acrylic floors, past other women on stools using old-fashioned handgrip telephones to talk to their incarcerated loved ones on the other side of glass panels.

"You will have thirty minutes to speak to the inmate," the guard said to Tati. Hearing the word *inmate* filled her with despair.

Handcuffed and accompanied by a guard, Huck entered a cell on the other side of the window. He half smiled at her while the guard unlocked the restraints. In a baggy gray prison jumpsuit, he looked like he'd lost weight, even though it'd been just over twenty-four hours since his arrest. He'd pulled his hair back and tied it into a stubby ponytail. He sat across from Tati, and she pressed one hand on the glass window between them. It was something she'd seen people do on true crime TV shows. She had also seen movies where women pressed their breasts against the window, flashing their titties as proof of their love. Tati wondered if she could slip one breast out of her bra discreetly enough so nobody other than Huck could see.

As if reading her mind, the guard at the end of the hall shot her an *I'm watching you* look. Meanwhile, Huck lifted the phone receiver on his side of the glass and gestured for Tati to take hers. "Oh, Huck," she sighed into the phone. "What's going on?"

Huck tapped on the window and showed her his phone, pointing at the correct end to speak into. Tati turned it upside down and tried again—she wanted to slap herself. *Could I look any more stupid?*

"Thanks for coming."

"What's it like in there?"

"Oh, it's not the Hotel LeVeque, but I've seen worse. Did I ever mention that I was arrested once before, in an act of civil disobedience during Occupy Columbus?"

"No, you never said. But Huck—killing Adam Erb wasn't just an act of civil disobedience."

Huck scratched his chin, as if contemplating this distinction for the first time.

Tati pressed for more information. "But are you okay? Has anybody hurt you?"

"Apart from being unjustly arrested, brutally interrogated, denied my rights, and forced to live in sordid, inhuman conditions, I'm fine."

Tati moaned, "That's horrible."

"True that. The American penal system is disgraceful. The facilities are practically medieval, with clogged urinals, gnats in the bunks, black mold growing in the drains, and a persistent yellow drip coming from the ceiling in my cell. I'd sooner bathe in bilgewater than use the shower here. The food is tasteless, not to mention devoid of nutritional value. However, my fellow prisoners are all decent enough folks. They call me 'professor' and ask me for legal advice. They're all innocent."

"All of them?"

"So they say."

"Do you believe them?"

"Oh, no," Huck said. "Only the black ones."

Tati worried that Huck was too preoccupied gathering sociological data to grasp the perilousness of his situation. "Why do they think you killed Adam Erb?"

Huck tsked. "The detective found my DNA at the crime scene. Purely circumstantial evidence."

"DNA is circumstantial?"

"If not circumstantial, exactly, then irrelevant. I inspected the crime scene, so it makes sense they found my DNA. But I was just helping. Personally, I think the Columbus police should hire more sociologists."

She agreed, although it sounded like Huck was more concerned about reforming the criminal justice system than proving his innocence.

"Is that all they have on you?" she asked.

"I admitted I disliked Adam Erb for being a bloodsucking capitalist. Detective Witt calls that motive."

"That's nothing. Lots of people hated him."

"She also claimed I blamed him for interfering with my research, and that I've held a grudge ever since he broke up the first great pay-it-forward streak at Drip 'n' Donuts. Remember? We came this close to breaking a world record." Huck showed just a sliver of space between his thumb and forefinger.

Tati remembered that day well. Her mother and Huck had both worked at Drip 'n' Donuts at the time. Specifically, she recalled when, at fifteen, she first laid eyes on Huck.

Tati withheld comment and tried to bring the conversation back onto point. "I'm 100 percent behind you. I want to help."

"Thank you. I'm going to get to the bottom of this. But I can't do it on my own. Tomorrow is my arraignment. Can you be in the courtroom for moral support?"

She liked the idea of supporting Huck, morally or otherwise. "Absolutely!"

The guard tapped his wristwatch, letting Huck know his time was nearly up.

"And one more thing...."

"Anything. Just ask."

Huck lowered his voice to almost a whisper. "Could you call my mother for me?"

Huck told himself to listen and show respect. Holding his tongue clashed with his well-honed contrariness when confronting authority. This predisposition served him well in academe, where intellectual rhetoric and scholarly discourse were survival skills; however, law-enforcement agents tended to view it unkindly, as they were hypersensitive to criticism. He had a hard time throttling his righteous indignation, though. In open Socratic debate, his logic would shred the prosecuting attorney's case like a verbal machete through the wet tissue paper of the law. If the stakes were lower than, well, life and death, he would dearly love to rain down all his liberal dudgeon upon them. Under the circumstances, though, with the death penalty on the table, this might not be the optimal time to unleash the full fury of his idealistic valor.

This is just an arraignment, he reminded himself. *Be nice.*

A clerk called out the docket number and bellowed, "All rise."

Huck's spirits deflated when the judge entered. He'd hoped for a black female judge, or at least a female one, preferably a millennial. Anybody but a Caucasian male boomer. Alas, the magistrate was an overweight, bald white man, around sixty years old, with beefy jowls, a double chin, and a potato nose. His black robes dragged the floor behind him, and when he sat behind the bench, they hung over him like a bedsheet. He looked more like the grim reaper than a fair adjudicator. At least he didn't wear a powdered wig.

The clerk shouted, "This is the arraignment for the case of *the People v. Hyun-ki Stanley Carp*, the Honorable Judge Fritz Steele presiding."

Huck winced at the mention of his full name.

While Judge Steele smoothed his robes and adjusted his chair, Huck peeked backwards. Tati and Ximena sat side by side in the first row of the public gallery. Tati held a cell phone, which livestreamed to Val, whose face filled the screen. Behind them Chavonne and Jay-Rome sat in the second row, and in the third row, across the aisle from each other, were Ginny Campbell and D'Nisha Glint, each with her own sketch artist. The only person beyond them was Detective Sally Witt, who stood in the rear next to the double doors.

Judge Steele cleared his throat and banged his gavel. He looked to the left and right of Huck. "Where is the defense counsel?"

Huck stepped to the side to intercept the judge's gaze. "I am representing myself." He crossed his arms. "Your Honorable."

The judge chuckled disdainfully, as if at an unfunny old joke. He began, "Son—"

Huck wanted to scream *I am not your son*, but refused to give him the satisfaction.

"The court strongly urges you to secure professional legal counsel. Abraham Lincoln said that a person who represents himself — "

"Has a fool for a client. Yes, I know. Although that adage originally derived from a fable translated and published by Sir Roger L'Estrange in 1692."

"Don't interrupt me!" the judge scolded.

"Facts are facts," Huck explained.

"Do not interrupt me with facts."

By Huck's reckoning, the judge interrupted *him*, not the other way around. Perhaps this was grounds for a mistrial? Except this was not, technically, a trial. Too bad — Huck much preferred for this whole affair to be over.

The judge continued, "Young man..."

Better to be called "young man" than "son," but still, Huck felt patronized.

"...this is a murder indictment. The trial will likely be quite complex. I strongly urge you to take advantage of your right to legal counsel. If you cannot afford a lawyer, the court will appoint one. However — "

Huck grimaced at the judge's tone. "I do not intend for this case to go to trial."

"Oh?"

"I intend to solve the crime," Huck declared.

Tati chirped "Yes" just loud enough for his ears only. Ximena, though, gasped "*¡Dios mio!*" loud enough for everybody in the courtroom to hear.

Judge Fritz Steele leaned forward on his elbows. "Oh? Please do solve the crime, so I can go home and watch the Judge Judy show."

"I don't know who that is, Your Honorable. I don't own a television."

"I was being facetious. Oh, never mind. Let's get on with this."

The judge nodded to the prosecutor, who had stood silently the whole time. Given a chance—at last—to speak, she tugged on her lapels and cut loose.

"Thank you, Your Honor. I am District Attorney Eliza Bender, representing the people of the great state of Ohio. The charges brought by the People against Mr. Carp are one count of aggravated homicide, one count of tampering with evidence, three counts of obstructing police business."

"*Three* counts of obstructing police business," Huck objected. "Puh-lease."

The judge asked, "You do realize you have the right to remain silent, don't you, Mr. Carp?"

"All that is required for evil to triumph is for good people to remain silent, Your Honorable."

"Edmund Burke?"

"Close. That was from John Stuart Mill, a great believer in the social necessity of justice in a democracy."

Eliza Bender nearly popped the top button on her blouse when she exclaimed, "Your Honor! The People do not need a civics lesson from Mr. Carp."

"Thank you," Judge Steele said, relieved to get back on script. "Now, Mr. Carp, how do you plead to these charges?"

"Not guilty, of course."

"Of course. Now, Ms. Bender, what conditions do the People seek for Mr. Carp's release on bail?"

"This murder was heinous in both its elaborate planning and brutal execution. The shocking violence committed against the victim, Adam Erb, staggers the People's sense of decency. Prudence thus dictates that the court protect society against such atrocities. Furthermore, any person capable of contriving this manner of crime is a likely flight risk. Therefore, the People request that Mr. Carp be *denied bail*."

The way that Ms. Bender amplified her words, *denied bail*, knocked Huck momentarily off balance, until moral backlash kicked in.

"That's absurd. I have no criminal record. I have lived in Ohio all my life. I am a member of the adjunct faculty of The Ohio State University. For crying out loud, I'm doing research on *altruism*. I deserve to be released on my own recognizance."

"This infamous case has aroused public outrage," Ms. Bender reminded the judge. "Mr. Carp's presence in the community would be dangerous to the people, as well as to himself."

"The *people*?" Huck scoffed. "I ought to know the people." He puffed his chest. "I am a sociologist."

"So you are," Judge Steele agreed. "Despite that, I will set your bail amount at one million dollars."

"One million dollars!" Huck protested. "I can't begin to raise that much money."

Tati leaned against Ximena's shoulder and started weeping. Chavonne grunted and shook her head. Jay-Rome ground his teeth.

"I can pay his bail," Val's voice rang out, via Tati's cell phone. "It's the least I can do for my pal."

Judge Steele looked around for the source of the voice, then, upon realizing where it came from, sighed and grumbled in the same breath.

"Thanks," Huck said to Val. "You're the best."

"I have one more condition," the judge broke in. "I concur with the People's contention that Mr. Carp should not freely mix with the community. I therefore further require that he be placed on monitored house arrest."

"Seriously?" Huck asked. "My home is a basement efficiency apartment in a quadruplex in the University District."

From the last row, a voice called, "Hyun-ki can to stay-uh at the home with me."

Huck swung around 180 degrees. He'd missed her when he glanced back earlier; she was so short that the backs of the seats in front of her had blocked her from view. Now, though, she hopped onto her seat, stomped her feet, and wagged a finger at the judge.

"I say. Hyun-ki is-ah innocent. He can be coming home with me, yaaah."

Huck crossed his arms over his ribs, as if to keep them from shattering. "*Mom?*" he gulped. "*You came!*"

CHAPTER 8

In their escalating battle for ratings, Ginny Campbell knew she had a wild card to play against D'Nisha Glint. A week before Adam Erb's murder, she had met him at his mansion to shoot an evening magazine segment on "Dream Cars of Central Ohio," featuring the Erb-mobile. Ginny had always wanted to take a spin in it, and Adam was pleased to oblige her. With Jay-Rome behind the wheel and Troll filming while riding shotgun, Ginny and Adam had stretched out in the back and drank long island iced teas while they embarked on a joyride through scenic Delaware County. Afterwards, Adam was as loath to let her go as she was to leave, so they repaired to the parlor of his mansion for a "nightcap," even though it was the middle of the afternoon. Sipping Valley Vineyards champagne while nibbling on smoked salmon and caviar canapés, they chatted "off the record" about Adam's favorite subject—himself. Little did Adam know that Ginny told Troll to keep the camera rolling.

She never planned to use that material, until Adam gave his de facto permission by dying. Death, like money, changes everything. Amid the hoopla following Adam's murder, Ginny realized that she was sitting on a bonanza of candid footage that would never be timelier than immediately. Given their ravenous appetite for Erb-abilia, her audience would devour it like jackals on filet mignon. She dubbed the piece "Adam Erb's Final Interview."

The best part was imagining D'Nisha Glint's furious reaction. She'd be so jealous she'd shit in her thong.

Ginny was working late, editing the footage for broadcast during prime time. It was eerie, seeing Adam so blithe and easygoing, not knowing at the time that within a week he'd die. But, in a way, that was quintessential Erb—thinking only about himself in the present tense.

Naturally garrulous when sober, Adam became a verbal fire hose after a few drinks. He also became shamelessly flirtatious. Ginny plied him with equal amounts of booze and flattery, building up to what she really wanted to ask him.

"Do you feel vindicated, Adam?"

"Why should I? I never did anything wrong."

"Some women accused you of pretty awful things."

Adam Erb was known for having a debonair smile and a sharp wit, but not so much for a sense of humor. In response to that statement, though, he started laughing convulsively. Ginny watched herself in the video and remembered how stunned she had been, even a little intimidated. The laughter came from his bowels and roiled in the back of his throat before bursting out in a hot, moist blast. It sounded like the diabolical chortle of a mustache-twirling villain, tying a maiden to railroad tracks in a cheesy old Western movie.

Reviewing the video, Ginny paused and zoomed in on his face. He looked like a clown without his makeup, revealing his true self.

The laughter dissolved into hyperventilating. When at length he caught his breath, Adam said, "Those women, I loved them all. Still do, despite our misunderstandings."

"Misunderstandings?"

"That's all it was." He uncrossed his legs and leaned forward to look Ginny in the eye. "I did nothing wrong. I'm a businessman. My product was lingerie. They were my models. I didn't hire them because of their brilliant minds or radiant personalities. They fooled themselves if they ever thought otherwise. Sex sells, always has and always will. They were sex workers when you get right down to it. Ain't capitalism grand?"

"Give the people what they want," Ginny commented.

"Exactly!" Adam pounced. "If the people want T & A, I'll give them T & A. So, don't you agree that I had a right to examine the products I purchased? If, for example — hypothetically speaking — I told one of my models that her breasts were drooping, wasn't that my prerogative? Under that circumstance, if I offered to massage her breasts, purely for the sake of rejuvenating their natural color and suppleness, I was merely offering a professional service, wasn't I? After all, I had thousands of dollars invested in the perkiness of her nipples. Allegedly."

Ginny watched her expression in the video. She impressed herself at how she urged him on with a subtle nod, which he seemed to take as approval. Adam thought he was smart, but she could play him like a banjo.

"And furthermore, as any good photographer will tell you, the model must be in the proper mood to sell the product. It would thus be reasonable and proper, wouldn't it, for me to offer to assist her with enhancing the mood?"

"How did you assist?" Ginny asked.

"Talking dirty to them, mostly."

"Just talking? That's it?"

"I'm fluent in the language of flirtation. Modesty aside, it seldom fails." Adam had a shit-eating smirk on his face. He slouched back into his chair, self-satisfied. "So, you see, it's preposterous to claim that I created sexual tension in the working environment, when the model's whole purpose was to sell sexual tension. Allegedly."

"Nevertheless," she said, making it sound like she was apologizing for bringing up the topic, "a few of those women made certain, uhm, unsavory accusations."

"Which were unsubstantiated and ultimately dropped," Adam pounced.

"Still, they took a toll on you."

Adam sighed. "Yes, I endured a difficult time. Painful as it was, it led me to a whole new career as a pundit podcaster. Although I lost many followers on social media, I slowly attracted new ones. People who said they understood me. People who called those women gold-diggers. People applauded me for exercising my right of free speech and standing up for free enterprise and American ingenuity. I eventually realized they were right. I was a victim of political correctness. The fake news media—present company excluded, Ginny—was out to get me.

"But I wasn't going to take it. I fought back. That's why I started *Talking Truth*. I say things that need to be said. My listeners trust me, because I say what they want to believe. Like you said — give the people what they want."

This is priceless, Ginny thought. *Testimony from the grave.* Until watching the video, she had forgotten what she asked him next.

"What about your accusers, Adam? What would be your final word to them?"

Adam put his chin on his rolled fist. "Thanks."

D'Nisha Glint kept asking until she found a lawyer who agreed with her. Adam Erb was dead. He left behind no will, no executor, no surviving family members, and no instructions whatsoever concerning the disposition of his wealth, businesses, or other proprietary interests. Despite having tens of thousands of friends on social media, he had few genuine human attachments. Probate courts would be busy for months, if not years, resolving claims on his estate. Lawyers representing dozens of clients already contended for a piece of the Erb pie. The first claim came within forty-eight hours of his death, from Barbara Knoop, his redneck one-night stand, who was suing for ten million dollars to support Adam's alleged unborn child. There would likely be other paternity claims. By dying, Adam Erb had created a litigious cash cow for countless rapacious lawyers.

Amid so much legal chaos, D'Nisha saw an opportunity. She argued that Adam's death invalidated his out-of-court settlements and non-disclosure agreements. Thus, the women whom he'd paid off could sue him posthumously for damages due to the severe emotional stress they suffered because of accepting Adam's hush money. They could double-dip on him, getting money *and* revenge.

D'Nisha contacted as many of Adam's accusers as she knew. For the most part, she didn't like them and they didn't like her, but that didn't matter, because animosity between models was a given. Though Adam referred to them collectively as the "Sisterhood of Erb," they constantly quarreled among themselves and ruthlessly competed to curry Adam's favor. Beauty and sex appeal, jealousy and backstabbing came with the modeling business as much as hairspray and body oil. Nevertheless, where money was concerned, D'Nisha presumed they would let bygones be bygones.

So, D'Nisha enlisted her erstwhile sisters to join her in a plot to get back at Adam and get rich in the process. There was Brooke, famous as the "avian darling," whose pictorial wearing raven feathers broke a million hearts and incited complaints from the SPCA. Lexi and Trixi, identical twins, who starred in the unveiling ceremony for Adam's Eve line of fig leaf lingerie. Clementine of the crotchless yoga pants, Cassidy of the spaghetti thong "skivvies," Yasmine of the edible licorice panties, and Ashanti of the lace straight jacket all answered D'Nisha's call. She told them she wanted to produce an exposé entitled "Adam Erb's Truth and Lies," and this was their chance to be heard — and to plead their cases for restitution.

The best part was Adam could do nothing to stop them.

Their stories shared several tawdry details. Ironically, when they were posing nearly nude on their backs in beds strewn with rose petals, Adam showed not so much as a wiggle of prurient interest. However, after the photo shoot, when they were fully clothed, he turned into a slavering horndog. He had some weird fetishes. He followed them into the women's restroom. He pretended he didn't know his fly was wide open. He snuck up behind them and sniffed their hair. He asked to kiss their hands and then licked their knuckles. He left a trail of green jellybeans for them to follow into his studio. Always, he drooled. These women were skilled in the art of rejecting the gauche sexual overtures of normal men. But Adam was a different kind of creep. He was their boss.

Also, it hadn't always been clear whether he intended to seduce them or play games with them. What can a girl do when her boss is a pubescent dweeb?

One after the other, D'Nisha interviewed her sisters and recorded their stories for the documentary. She teared up in sympathy when they described the angst and humiliation they suffered because of Adam Erb. She handed them tissues when they broke down weeping. Sure, they were fashion models, paid to be objectified, but that didn't mean they didn't have feelings too. Adam made them feel "icky," "gross," "gnarly," and "skuzzy." Even though they accepted hush money from him, the payout did not relieve them of an oppressive shame, for which they felt entitled to additional compensation.

D'Nisha didn't stop there, though. She learned from other sources that Adam had engaged the services of prostitutes following his fall from grace. She tried to interview dancers from the Booti Tooti Club, where he often solicited female companionship, but none of the ladies would speak to her. "The men who come here need and expect privacy," the bouncer, Tank Turner, grumbled to her. When Turner slammed the door in her face, it was great theater.

In her conclusion, D'Nisha said, "Nobody knew the *real* Adam Erb. He was a hero to some, but he was also a slave to his hidden dark side. His wealth concealed but did not excuse his behavior. He was famous for 'talking truth,' except when the subject was himself.

"He prospered by speaking the truth, but every word of it was a lie."

Touché! D'Nisha congratulated herself. She was so proud of that last line that she had her lawyer look into getting it trademarked.

D'Nisha aired her documentary on Sunday evening, immediately after Ginny Campbell's sleazy little tête-à-tête interview with Adam. She considered it a double win—humiliation for Adam and ratings for her.

Detective Sally Witt was not in the mood to go home. Alone in her office in the precinct, she watched "Adam Erb's Final Interview" with Ginny Campbell in its entirety. She started watching D'Nisha Glint's exposé, "Adam Erb's Truth and Lies," but turned it off halfway through, and then turned it back on for the last five minutes. She couldn't resist, even though she doubted that either of those vacuous bimbos knew half as much about Erb as she did. After all, she had been lead investigator into his sexual misconduct, only to close the case abruptly when his victims withdrew their complaints. Nevertheless, even though her captain told her to drop it, she had continued to unofficially work the case. The deeper she looked into Adam Erb, the more the machinations of his mind fascinated and appalled her. She subscribed to the *Talking Truth* podcast, and not only found that she agreed with most of his rants, but found his blunt non-politically correct rhetoric to be refreshing. He was a macho, blustery, knuckle-dragging philanderer with his brain in his dick, but that didn't make him wrong.

The television in Sally's office was a six-inch black-and-white portable, which she had bought from Radio Shack back in college. It was the only TV she'd ever owned in her life. Sally's office was a storage room where she claimed squatter's rights. It smelled rank from mildew and was infested with cockroaches, which she joked were her pets. The walls were unpainted windowless cinder blocks, which were cold and damp even in summer. Her desk, which she'd rescued from the department's surplus warehouse, was made of gray steel. It had two drawers—one that got stuck, and the other that never closed properly. She sat on a rolling desk chair with one wheel that didn't turn. Stacked photocopy paper boxes served as her filing cabinet. The floor was black-and-white checkered linoleum; exposed, rusted pipes crossed the ceiling; and the only light came from a sixty watt bulb, which dangled from a frayed cord. It was more suitable as a cell for solitary confinement than an office, but she liked it. Nobody bothered her when she closed her door.

Sally was more than just a passive observer to Ginny Campbell and D'Nisha Glint's competing docudramas; she tested her Erb instincts against theirs. When Ginny Campbell posed him a question, Sally imagined herself observing and listening to Adam Erb through Ginny's eyes and ears. She tried to anticipate Ginny's reactions and follow-up questions. She inventoried Adam Erb's body language, from his twitchy pinky finger to the way his Adam's apple jumped when he didn't like the question. She felt tacit sexual gameplay between them. When Ginny asked, "Do you feel vindicated, Adam?" she did so with a rising inflection, sort of like prostitute's solicitation: Hey there, mister. Want to feel *vindicated* tonight? Then when Adam answered, "I did nothing wrong," he sounded like a cheating lover who didn't care if he was believed, so long as he could avoid a fight. Sally wondered if Ginny and Adam had ever fucked. If not, too bad for them. There was enough latent sexual energy between them to launch a rocket.

Sally had less empathy for D'Nisha Glint. She was too self-consciously gorgeous to be taken seriously. Halfway through "Adam Erb's Truth and Lies," Sally turned it off.

In the silence, she stood and faced her crazy board, from enough distance to take it all in at once. After initially cutting and pasting and tying threads between dozens of pieces, she had not added another item since Huck Carp's arrest. That bothered her — not because she didn't have enough evidence to convict that smart-alecky little professor, but because the story of Adam Erb's murder deserved a larger stage with more characters and twisty-turning subplots. So, she tacked photos of Ginny Campbell and D'Nisha Glint to opposite sides of the board and ran a long twine between them, then back to Adam. If nothing else, those two bitches were guilty of character assassination.

Sally turned the program back on in time to see D'Nisha Glint conclude by saying, in a poker-faced closeup, "Nobody knew the *real* Adam Erb." Sally Witt disagreed. She knew him. She had compiled a long checklist of his flaws and foibles: Adam Erb was narcissistic — check; Adam Erb was pompous — check; Adam Erb was wanton — check; Adam Erb was greedy, grabby, tactless, demanding, impatient, insensitive, irascible, insatiable, and sometimes just downright weird — check and double check all of those boxes, and more.

Sexy as hell — check?

When Detective Witt became the Erb case's lead investigator, she'd felt like she'd won the lottery. Investigating Adam Erb's sex crimes promised to be stimulating. She looked forward to getting Adam across the table from her in the interrogation room. But his accusers peremptorily dropped their complaints — obviously, he'd bought them out. Too damn bad, because she would have loved a chance to look him in the eye and ask him dirty questions.

When the show finished, Sally pulled the plug on the TV. She stared at the blank screen; it somehow captured her feelings.

She really should go home. It had been five years since she and Duke divorced, yet she still dreaded being home alone, in part because it was lonely, but more because she feared that one day, when she least expected it, he would show up on her doorstep, drunk and belligerent, or drunk and remorseful, or drunk and horny—in any case, drunk was a given—and, in a moment of concupiscent weakness, she might let him in. Even though she had purged everything of his from the residence, Duke remained a pervasive presence there. Going home was like poking a sleeping ghost; she was paying mortgage on a haunted house. She would have moved into her office if only there was a shower available.

Sally reached into the bottom drawer of her file cabinet, where instead of hiding a bottle like TV cops always did, she kept her secret stash of private reading materials. After she'd resumed reading from where she'd marked the page, the door to her office groaned open. Simultaneously, the ringtone sounded on her phone. She jolted onto her feet, shaking, as if tased from behind.

"Witt! What th' fuck all 're you still here for?" her captain asked, entering the room.

Sally stuffed her reading material back into the drawer. "Hey, hey captain. Just tying together ends. But I'm just about ready to call it a day."

"I see," the captain said, lingering on the hard *e* sound. He moved his eyes side to side without budging his head. "Good."

Sally waited for the captain to leave, then checked her cell phone. She had a new text. It was from *Adam Erb*.

Sally looked up, as if she expected to see him standing there. In the shadowy corner of her office, the coat stand seemed to take human shape.

"I like you better dead," Sally said.

When the coat stand failed to answer, she extended her middle finger, then swiped it across the screen to open the text message. It read, *Kill me once, shame on you. Kill me twice, shame on me. Kill me thrice, shame on us.*

"Fuck me three times," Sally Witt said to herself. Adam Erb might be dead, but he nonetheless lived and thrived in digital form. Within minutes, Sally observed that three new hashtags — #KillMeOnce, #KillMeTwice, and #KillMeThrice — were trending in Columbus. Apparently, she was not the only person to receive that same text message from Adam Erb.

In life, Adam Erb had gotten the best of her; in death, he taunted her; in between, he annoyed her with junk email. Sally wished she did have a bottle in the drawer of her file cabinet like all those TV cops. She really wanted a stiff drink.

CHAPTER 9

At first, home confinement as a condition of bail sounded to Huck like an ideal situation. He had time to work on his research, apply for grants, catch up on sociological literature, *and* solve Adam Erb's murder, all free from the niggling distractions of the real world. It was the next best thing to a sabbatical. Upon hearing the judge's decree, Huck blurted out "thank you" and gestured namaste toward him. The judge slammed his gavel with malice, as if he knew something that Huck didn't.

In retrospect, Huck should have kept his mouth shut. He'd been hasty when he objected to serving house arrest in his apartment; it was minuscule, but at least it had a WiFi connection, unlike the Carp family farm, some seventy miles north of Columbus in rural Knox County. On top of that, Detective Witt confiscated his computer, cell phone, and filing cabinet as "evidence." Huck pleaded with her that the only information she would find in them was data on the purchase and consumption of donuts, but his protests were to no avail. Finally, in perhaps the cruelest blow, the judge required him to wear an ankle monitor, which would send an inaudible electronic alarm to the authorities if he strayed more than a couple hundred yards beyond Carp property. Even the cattle were permitted to roam farther than that.

Huck had never felt like he belonged on the farm. In abstract, he approved of family farms. Farming was a noble profession. He sympathized with the plight of family farmers, an oppressed class abused by corporate agribusiness. But, unfortunately, actual farmers tended to be hicks, rubes, rednecks, and hillbillies, none more so than his own family. In the seven years since leaving for college, he'd returned to the Carp family homestead only once, for his father's funeral. Even then, he snuck out of the wake early, before his older brothers got drunk and started singing "Sweet Home Alabama," as was their wont.

Fortunately, his brothers were currently snowbirding on their annual expedition to Orlando where, in their own words, they were on a "pussy-hunting" expedition. Those two were enough to give the putatively "Happiest Place on Earth" a bad name. Huck suspected they were closeted gay. That left Huck alone with his mother until the trial.

She told him, "If you-uh, want the anything, please just to ask."

"Okay, Mom," he answered. That seemed doable; to avoid talking to her, he just wouldn't ask for anything.

Later that afternoon, she repeated the offer, this time adding, "I make you-uh, the sandwich. Peanut butter and jelly."

"No thank you. I'm allergic to peanut butter."

"Okay, so. I make only the jelly sandwich. No crusts. Like you-uh, like."

"I'm not hungry," he said. His stomach rumbled.

"You see. You need eat," his mother said.

Indeed, he *was* hungry. "Maybe later," he said and left the room.

As he rounded the corner, he heard his mother mutter, "Don't be asshole."

Unlike his brothers, who thrived on her largesse, Huck felt ambivalent about accepting favors from his mother. In fact, she made him feel ambivalent about his whole existence. In 1985, his mother, Eun Sook Kim of Seoul, met and married Stanley Carp of Danville, Ohio, thirty years her senior, both on the same day. They agreed to matrimony on the sole basis of letters and photos they'd exchanged over a period of one month. She took the American name of Eunice. They immediately set about spawning children. The arrangement benefited them both.

To Huck, though, the transaction smacked of colonialism. Despite the sad irony of it, Huck disapproved of the very union that had brought him into this world.

That evening, Eunice drove into Mount Vernon and bought a bucket of extra-crispy Clucky Fried Chicken for their dinner. "It good," she insisted and bit into a drumstick.

The inside of the bucket was wrapped in wax paper, which was mottled with greasy spots and crumbs that stuck to it like boogers. Huck, who never ate deep-fried foods, felt poisoned just watching her. Not wishing to trigger an argument, though, he grabbed a spork and took a bite of the coleslaw that came as a side dish.

"Allergic, too, eating chicken?" his mother asked.

"I'm eating light," he said.

"You-uh too skinny. Need some to eat real food." She waved the drumstick in front of his nose, which stirred his indigestion even more.

"Please, no, Mom."

With her hands on her hips, she fumed, "You-uh don't like my cooking?"

"You call this cooking?"

"Pppppf-uck you, Hyun-ki."

Huck could not abide his mother cursing, even though, given her accent, when she dropped an f - bomb it sounded more like a dud firecracker fizzling than an expletive. He imagined that cursing in English must be very frustrating for her.

"All right, already." Huck snatched an extra-crispy wing from the bucket and chomped into it.

Huck was up most of that night on the toilet purging his bowels. In between episodes of extreme gastrointestinal distress, Huck realized that if he was going to survive house arrest in the boondocks with his mother, he needed to keep busy. Unable to sleep, he decided to make a to do list. Item number one: Make a Plan. That wasn't very clarifying, though, so he puzzled for a few minutes before jotting down: Get a Computer.

The next morning, over breakfast of sausage and grits, he asked his mother, "Do you have a computer?"

"Sure. The boys, they-uh have one. I not know nothing about how to using it, though."

"Do you know the password?"

"Password."

"Yes, what's the password?"

"Yaaaah. That's the password. Password. You-uh see?"

Of course. He should have guessed.

Huck was afraid of what he might find on the computer. It was a luggable old Dell laptop; the keyboard was tacky to the touch; the X key was missing. He was curious but dared not open the file folder labeled Meat. Nevertheless, the laptop was his lifeline to the world, and Huck was glad to have it. He clicked on the network icon and saw only two networks within range, neither stronger than a single bar.

"What's the name of your network?" he asked his mother.

"Net-what? You-uh mean the Internet?"

"Yes. The connection seems weak. Where's the router?"

"I no need Internet." She lifted her chin proudly. "Waste of time."

For the first time since his arrest, Huck started to panic. "No Internet? But I need it. Mom, please."

"What for the ppppfff-uck?" she asked dismissively, but then softened when she saw the look of trepidation on Huck's face. "The boys. They-uh sometimes using the neighbor's net-uh-work. They take computer to the barn; they say it's getting the better reception here."

"That's just great."

So, even though the temperature outside was in the single digits and snow was blowing and drifting so hard as to make the distance between the house and the barn seem like an arctic demilitarized zone, Huck packed up the laptop, smothered himself in a coat and scarf, and trudged through hostile elements in search of a functional network connection. The wind whipped tiny shards of snow crystals that felt like shrapnel hitting his cheeks. He pushed once, twice, and a third time, finally sweeping aside enough snow to wedge through the barn door. Once inside, he shook himself free of the gathered snow.

"Gggggyyyyuuuukkkkk, quurt quurt!"

Huck envisioned a Sasquatch breathing down his neck. He dropped the computer and scrambled halfway up the ladder into the hayloft before he turned to see what kind of demonic abomination had bellowed at him so fiercely.

Elvis Pigsley, a 250-pound barrow hog, stuck its hairy snout between the slats of its pen and greeted Huck with another gut-wrenching eructation. It reminded him of his brothers after a night of hard drinking.

"Good swine," he said. "Don't mind me. I'm just here to use the Internet."

To which the agreeable hog replied, "Soooooooeeeeeeey."

Tati read Huck's email over and over, imagining that he'd written it on scented parchment and sealed it with a kiss.

"Here at the farm, I have sketchy Internet access and can't get the resources I need for my investigation," he wrote to her. "I need your help, or I'm screwed."

Tati liked the idea that Huck, feeling "screwed," reached out to her. She wasn't trying to be coy when she replied, "I'll do anything you ask," but he could freely interpret those words however he wished.

What he wanted, specifically, was for her to help gathering facts and tracking down leads to prepare his defense. "I need people I can trust," he wrote, and urged her to ask for other trustworthy volunteers to join his "defense team."

Unfortunately, Tati's closest friends all possessed big mouths and could not keep a secret to save their lives. Most of the time, she liked that about them — she appreciated good gossip as much as the next girl. But she did not want them flapping their tongues about Huck.

Ditto that, concerning her mother. Ximena offered to help without even being asked, which was sweet of her, but the last thing Tati wanted was for Ximena to chaperone her. Tati needed to follow the clues wherever they led. This case was X-rated, and Tati worried about explaining some of the subtler points of sadomasochism to her mother — not that she was personally acquainted with them, herself... but, well, she'd read *Fifty Shades of Gray*, like everybody else.

Huck suggested she reach out to Val Vargas, and Tati was glad for that. Val was fun, in an airheaded but ingenious sort of way. When Tati told her that Huck needed help, she was flattered to think that he valued her skills so highly. "I'm all in," she vowed.

The two of them, though, hardly constituted a "team." At work, Tati drummed her fingers on the counter, pondering her next move.

Chavonne snapped her fingers in front of Tati's face, interrupting her daydream. "Yo. Earth to Tati. Wake up, girl."

"Huh?"

"I know that look on yo' face. It's 'bout Huck, ain't it?"

"No," she said, acting upon a knee-jerk instinct to deny. She had in fact been thinking about Huck, but it unnerved her that Chavonne had read her thoughts.

"Have yo' heard from him?"

"He's... in trouble."

"No shit. That boy is too smart for his own good. What he needs is some street smarts."

"Like you?" Tati asked.

"Damn straight like me. I could really help that boy, if he'd let me."

"Really? Do you mean that?"

"I don't say nothin' I don't mean."

Tati felt a twinge of hesitation. Chavonne was her boss, but on this team, Tati felt like she should be in charge. "Ok, then," she said at length. "Huck needs our help."

While Tati and Chavonne mulled over how they might aid Huck, a voice from the other side of the counter butted in. "I might be able to help some too."

While they'd been talking, Jay-Rome, sitting in a booth quietly drinking coffee and munching a devil's food donut, had eavesdropped on their conversation. Tati bristled. She hardly knew him, so why was he butting into their conversation?

"He's cool," Chavonne vouched for Jay-Rome. "He can help. Nobody knew Adam Erb better than Jay-Rome."

"So, okay then," Tati agreed with Chavonne's point. "Thanks. Both of you. So, listen, if you really want to help Huck, we need to set up a meeting of the whole team."

That evening, Tati, Chavonne, and Jay-Rome sat around the table in the Drip 'n' Donuts manager's office. Val joined them via Chavonne's laptop; she sat in a beanbag chair eating Cheetos. They all stared at Tati's cell phone, waiting for it to ring.

"Yo' sure Huck's goin' t' call?" Chavonne asked. "It's done past seven o'clock."

"Yes. I am 100 percent positive sure," Tati insisted, although she worried because it was unlike him to be late. Furthermore, he'd told her that he'd been getting death threats. What if...?

Everybody jumped when Tati's cell started playing "Livin' La Vida Loca."

"Ooops. That's my ringtone," she explained, blushing.

"Answer it, befo' I get that song stuck in my brain," Chavonne implored her.

Tati complied. "Hello? Huck? Is that you?"

The voice on the other end sounded like it shouted from the bottom of a well. "Hellooooooooo."

"We can't hear you."

"Sorry." They heard a rapping. "Can you hear me now?"

Everybody chimed in, "Yes."

"You're on speaker phone," Tati said.

"Sorry. I can't get decent reception out here on the farm, so I'm using my mother's ancient dial-up phone. You practically have to shout to be heard."

"I've never seen one of those kinds of phone," Val piped in. "I didn't think they could still work."

"It feels like talking into a tin can."

Tati steered the conversation back on subject. "The whole team is here. Me, Chavonne, Val, and Jay-Rome — remember him, the limo driver? We're ready to help. What can we do?"

"That's great. Listen to me. I need something from each of you. This is important." They heard papers shuffling. "Okay, then. Val? Are you there?"

"Yessir, Huck. I'm here. Well, not literally here, but virtually. Anyhow — what can I do for you?"

"I need to keep up with social media. What's trending right now?"

"Let's see. Currently, trend numero uno is #DangERB, as in *Adam was a #DangERB to women everywhere*. It launched after D'Nisha Glint's stupid exposé. Did you see that? It sucked. But the second hottest trend is #SuffERB, like *Adam #SuffERB for telling the truth*. Ginny Campbell gave the hashtag some oomph by retweeting it."

"Hmmmm," Huck mused. "Are any of the older hashtags still hot?"

"Oh, yeah. #PutERBtoBedWet is still hanging around in the top five. Nobody really knows exactly what it means, but that's part of its staying power. And of course, Madame Secsy keeps delivering her #ProvERBs, like:

> *#ProvERB68. Beauty is in the eye of the abuser.*
> *#ProbERB69. Do your own thing, but if you must, do it alone.*

I've created a folder for them. They're priceless. She may want to publish them in a book someday. By now, she's probably up to eighty."

"Interesting," Huck mulled. "Have you ever met her, Val?"

Val tsked. "Nobody meets Madame Secsy. She's like an Internet bodhisattva, who exists on another plane of being. We only know her by social media."

"Interesting." The static over the phone seemed to reflect Huck's thought processes. "I need to get in touch with her. But I can't do it myself. Could you, Val?"

"Not possible." Val paused. "But she does personally contact every new member with an individual welcome message. It's quite an honor, because not everybody makes the cut."

"Really," Huck said, then pivoted. "Chavonne...?"

"Yo' Huck."

"Would you please apply to join the Society of Enlightened Celibates?"

"Fo' real? I don't think I qualify. I mean, sure, I done kicked out Eldridge's lazy ass, and right now I'm sick and tired of men in gen'ral. But ain't that kind of extreme?"

"It's not so bad," Val jumped in.

Huck answered, "You don't have to go through with actually doing it — or *not* — as the case may be. All I ask is that you forward that welcome message to me."

"Whew." Chavonne wiped her brow. "If tha's all yo' want, I'll do it."

"Excellent," Huck commended her, then called out, "Jay-Rome? Are you there too?"

Jay-Rome gulped down a large bite of devil's food donut. "Hey up, bruh. I'm on board. Besides, ain't like I got a job now anyhow."

"Good. I need a favor from you. What can you tell me about when you drove Adam Erb to the Booti Tooti Club?"

"Well, I ain't no snitch, but seeing as how he's dead... I guess it's copacetic. I don't rightly know how many times I took him there. Half a dozen, maybe.

He'd go in, stay for an hour or two while I chilled in the parking lot, then after he got his fill of whatever, he'd come out and I'd take him home. 'Xcept for the last time. He brought a lady with him back to the limo. I don't know what happened, because he drew the curtains. Usually, that meant the limo was about to start rockin'. Not that night, though. About fifteen minutes later, she let herself out. She was laughing, but it weren't a funny laugh—more like a nasty one. And clouds of smoke rolled out when she opened the door. It stank like tear gas. After that, the boss man was white like a sheet—he told me to drive him home. The weirdest thing, though, was that when I parked the limo in the garage, he didn't get out. I asked him if he was okay, but he just told me to leave and not to mention nothing about what happened that night. Since I didn't know what happened, that was easy to do. Until now, that is."

"Interesting." The sound of Huck's fingers tapping on a keyboard could be heard over the speaker. "What did this woman look like?"

"Uh, well." Jay-Rome tugged on the collar of his shirt. "She looked naked."

"Did she have any conspicuously identifying features?"

"Excuse me for saying so, ladies." Jay-Rome nodded at Tati and Chavonne. "But I mostly remember her humongous boobies? They looked like bumper cars on her chest."

"I need more information," Huck said. "Will you go back there for me? Ask for Nadine and tell her that you want to see her act?"

"Can do, bruh."

"I need details."

A long pause followed, as each member of the team imagined what those details might look like.

Tati couldn't take the silence one second longer. "Huck, are you still there?"

"I'm thinking. It's hard, without the Internet."

"Of course. We will do anything we can to help you," Tati promised. "But...."

"What?"

"Everybody else is doing something. What can *I* do to help?"

"I was getting to that," Huck replied quickly. "I need for you to betray me...."

Living on a chauffeur's salary, Jay-Rome could not afford to frequent gentleman's clubs. On special occasions, when he did seek the kinds of pleasures those venues provided, he adhered to high standards. No dives, please. Some dudes went slumming in dank holes where garish neon flashing lights promised GIRLS, GIRLS, GIRLS. Jay-Rome avoided those places.

By contrast, he looked for legitimate adult cabarets that advertised their elegance with subdued exterior lighting, tinted windows above eye level, a solid door with ornate patterns, and a well-lit parking lot filled with tricked-out late-model cars. The best joints even featured valet parking. He appreciated a place where he could fit in while wearing a white felt fedora, cashmere jacket, and riotous bling. He felt comfortable in a club where the interior had subtle perimeter lighting, open spaces for roaming, a bar with chrome rails and plush stools, and a central stage like a theater in the round, although with a pole. Among his fellow gentlemen, he could switch between casting admiring glances at the athleticism of the dancers and carrying on lively conversations about the day's affairs. Of course, drop dead gorgeous waitresses clad only in glitter welcomed him with a sweet smile and called him by his first name. Even the food was good.

The Booti Tooti Club was *not* one of those places. It not only fell far below Jay-Rome's usual standards for a gentleman's club, but it failed even to meet his minimal hygienic expectations. Standing in the parking lot, in fearful anticipation of what awaited him behind those rusty metal doors, Jay-Rome tried to recall when he'd had his last tetanus shot.

To enter, he had to walk by a huddle of slobs, rednecks, and seedy degenerates smoking and spitting tobacco outside the door. There wasn't a single brother in the whole lot of them. He felt their sloppy drunk glares burn on the back of his neck. Once inside, his sinuses shrank from breathing air thickened by heavy breathing and hormonal excretions. Lonely men sat at rickety tables by themselves, their hands out of view. On stage, the nude woman writhed for their amusement while hanging from a pole. Floodlights beat down on her like lighthouse beacons. She had a detached look on her face. Jay-Rome wondered what she was thinking—did she imagine herself as a fashion model prancing on a Parisian walkway? Or, was she merely going through the motions, devoid of thought or imagination. He felt sorry for her, sorry for the men, and sorry for himself for being there.

"'Sup, buddy? There's a two drink minimum," the beefy man at the end of the bar said to him.

"Are you Tank?" Jay-Rome asked. God help him if he was wrong and had just called somebody *Tank*. He'd heard that rednecks battled over far less.

"Who's asking?" the man demanded.

"My name's Jay-Rome. My friend Huck Carp said I should ask for Tank."

"Huckster?" The man relaxed his jowls. "How's the kid holding up?"

"He's been better."

"No shit. Tell him if he needs to unwind while waiting on his trial, he can come here. Lap dances on the house. Me'n the girls all think Huck is badass for butchering that pervert Adam Erb. I couldn't have sliced and diced him up any better my own self."

Jay-Rome resisted the inclination to defend Huck's innocence. "That's dope, man," he said noncommittally.

"So, any friend of Huck is a friend of the Booti Tooti Club. What can I do yah for?"

Jay-Rome had practiced in the mirror so he could look sincere when he said, "Huck told me I should ask for a private show from Nadine."

"Well dip me in shit and jam a Popsicle stick up my ass," Tank chortled. "Huck said that, did he? I don't recall him partaking of Ms. Nadine's services when he dropped by on Valentine's Day. But it doesn't matter, I'm touched. In this business, word of mouth is the best advertising."

Jay-Rome wondered how literally to take that phrase,"word of mouth."

Sparse applause and a few hoots and guffaws interrupted them as Nadine L'Amour finished her dance. She took a long bow with her legs spread wide, wiggled her hips, then dropped onto her hands and knees like a dog to retrieve the loose change and dollar bills men tossed at her. When she'd scooped up all the cash, she shimmied over to Tank and handed everything to him.

"Cheap motherfuckers," Nadine griped.

Tank counted the money, putting half into the cash register and returning half to Nadine. "Don't let those cocksuckers get you down. This night is just getting started." He stepped aside to let Nadine size up Jay-Rome, and vice versa.

"Well, well. Who is this hot stud?" she purred.

Jay-Rome didn't want to divulge his name. "I'm an admirer."

"This here gentleman asked for you upon the recommendation of our buddy, Huckster. He wants to view your private show."

"I'd be pleased to oblige." Nadine pulled Jay-Rome by the zipper. "Come with me into the VIP lounge."

Jay-Rome followed through a waterfall of beaded curtains into a room the size of a walk-in closet. Nadine urged him to make himself comfortable in an overstuffed chair covered with pink velvet upholstery. He sank deep into the cushion, which smelled like the kind of cheese kept under glass. Although thoroughly disgusted, he was also solidly aroused.

"Make yourself comfortable." She eyed his erection. "There's no need to be shy with me."

Huck had instructed Jay-Rome to get facts, nothing more, then to report back everything that happened. First, though, he had to survive.

Nadine sat in a well-oiled leather vinyl papasan chair. She stretched and rolled in it until her skin gleamed with a thin film of lubrication. Next to the papasan was a plastic end table, on top of which was a box of obscenely large cigars. Nadine took one and rolled it over her body from her chest to her thighs.

"Are you ready?" she asked him.

"I don't know. What's ready?"

"Uhmmmm. Didn't your friend tell you what to expect?"

"Not really."

"Then you are in for a rare treat. This performance is exclusive to the Booti Tooti Club. My friend, Sybil Exxxotica, taught it to me, and she learned it from a Vietnamese nun. But she doesn't perform any more. So, I am the one and only."

"Do I, uh, do anything?"

"Do whatever moves you. But most men just watch."

That was a relief. Jay-Rome sank his head onto a pillow and adjusted his belt so he could watch with three eyes.

"Open wide," Nadine said and inserted the cigar into Jay-Rome's mouth so deep he felt it scratch the back of his throat. "Suck good and hard."

He needed to suck hard just to breathe. While Jay-Rome drooled over half of the cigar, Nadine clipped the other half and struck a match with her fingernail. She held the match to the clipped end and encouraged Jay-Rome to "puff, honey, puff." He sucked and puffed until he'd stoked a bright red ember. When Nadine removed the cigar from his mouth, he exhaled knots of rank greenish smoke. He felt on the brink of passing out.

"Good job," Nadine congratulated him. "If you can light it, I can smoke it."

Facing Jay-Rome, Nadine uncoiled in the papasan. She planted her feet on the floor and lifted her hips and butt to Jay-Rome's eye level, then opened her knees to a broad obtuse angle, with her bushy genitalia at its axis.

"Ay, ay, ay, auuuuuh," Nadine panted.

Nadine slowly guided the cigar lower against her body until she inserted it into the glistening cleft between her legs. The cigar's ember flared. When she withdrew it, a serpentine rope of smoke rose from within and spread into the shape of a valentine heart above her. One heart after another drifted over Jay-Rome's head, then descended around his neck like a ring of Hawaiian leis.

Nadine rolled onto her side and then looked back over her shoulder at Jay-Rome. "Was it good for you too?"

Every pore on Jay-Rome's body was engorged, except for where it mattered. Down there, his erstwhile erection had shrank like a scared rabbit hiding in its hole.

Nadine pulled on a robe. "Okay. Show's over."

Jay-Rome's teeth started to chatter. His heartbeat thumped in the back of his throat, as if his epiglottis was a punching bag.

Nadine left him alone in the room. "Hey, Tank," she called. "You'd better get the oxygen tank. We got another one needing resuscitation."

"Ain't nobody's fuckin' business," Chavonne railed. "And I sho' as hell don't think it's smart puttin'

such information 'bout myself on the goddamned Internet."

Watching her via WhatsApp, Val said, "Don't take it personally. The point is to test an applicant's honesty. Just answer the questions truthfully."

"I get it," Chavonne conceded. "But if I answer that question in all truth, then I got to say 'I don't know.'"

"Really? How's that possible?"

That was the problem. Whenever Chavonne tried to recall getting down and dirty with Eldridge or Leon or Clarence or any of her other recent boyfriends, she drew a blank. What she did remember, though, were times when she rebuffed their romantic overtures. Horny dudes could be kind of disgusting, all groping and slobbering like hound dogs.

Chavonne was ready to hit Ctrl+Alt+Del and give up. "I'm sorry. I just can't."

Tati rescued her by saying, "That's okay. I can't remember, either."

Chavonne doubted that was true, but even so it confirmed her suspicion that she hadn't slept with Huck. Damn, what was wrong with that boy!?!

"Tha's too bad, girl," she said. "Yo' is too young 'n' hot not to be getting some action."

Val bristled visibly over the cell phone. "Okay, then. Just answer 'I don't know.'"

Chavonne clicked the appropriate box and proceeded. It seemed like she had to provide more personal information to apply for membership in the Society of Enlightened Celibate Savants than to her gynecologist. She hadn't taken it seriously when Val warned her that the Society conducted "extreme vetting" on all applicants. It didn't comfort her that Val offered to help with the application, nor that she promised to "put in a good word" on her behalf. It didn't make sense that she would need an endorsement to get into a club that nobody wanted to belong to.

On the other hand, Chavonne was glad that Tati was there. While Val's support felt like judgment, Tati's felt like empathy.

"I don't get it, why fo' they axkin' my sexual preference. Ain't the whole point that yo' ain't s'posed to have none, anyhow?"

"Not so," Val corrected. "Being celibate doesn't mean you aren't sexually attracted to men, women, or both."

"Huh?" Chavonne and Tati asked simultaneously.

"Take me, for example." Val pointed at herself. "I'm a passionate heterosexual. I just love dicks. Big ones, thick ones, stiff ones, floppy ones, crooked ones, circumcised or uncircumcised, even little mousy ones."

Chavonne waited for a punch line. Maybe this SECS business was just an elaborate prank to punk unsuspecting victims. At any moment, she expected some lily-white game show host with a bright shit-eating grin would pop out from behind a fake wall and yell, *gotcha!*

Val relented. "Sorry," she said. "I get carried away sometimes. I probably shouldn't have said that."

"So, if yo' like dicks so much, why fo' did yo' join up with these wallflowers?"

"Passion is energy," Val explained. "SECS encourages its members to flirt, tease, fantasize, and even touch ourselves. It's all good, because it generates metabolic energy, which fuels the body and elevates the mind. By turning stored sexual energy inward, the most advanced SECS members experience a sensation called an *injaculation*."

"What's that like?" Chavonne asked.

"I'm sorry, but I can't tell you. It's way too complex for you to understand unless you've worked the program."

"Bullshit!" Chavonne snapped. "If not havin' sex gives a person superpowers, then by now I ought to be Wonder fuckin' Woman."

Tati laughed. The bottom of Val's head sank below the monitor, so only her eyes showed.

"All right. I'm just messin' with yo'," Chavonne laughed. "I'll check that I'm bisexual. I really think I might be. So there. Now, what's the next question?"

Val shrugged. "You need to provide references."

They found Detective Witt sitting in the break room with a cold coffee and half-eaten Twinkie on the table in front of her. She was staring at her cell phone, flipping through screen after screen as if looking for something. Thus preoccupied, the detective was unaware when they entered the room. Tati felt like it'd be rude to interrupt her, but the man who had escorted her into the precinct called in a growly voice, "Can you spare a moment, detective?"

Detective Witt jerked as if startled and sighed as if irritated, both at once. She closed the open app on her cell phone, turned, and said, "Good morning, captain."

The captain pointed to Tati. "I believe you're acquainted with Ms. Gonsalves."

"Sure. Toni, right? No, that's not it. Tori?"

"It's Tati. Remember? I work at Drip 'n' Donuts. You asked me a bunch of questions...."

"Yeah, yeah. 'Course I remember. You're Huck Carp's girlfriend, ain't you?"

Tati fought to refrain from smiling when the detective referred to her as Huck's "girlfriend," even though the detective's surly tone sounded disapproving.

"Ms. Gonsalves has some information about the Erb case," the captain intervened. "And she insists on speaking only to you."

"Is that so?" Detective Witt stuffed the rest of the Twinkie in her mouth and continued speaking while chewing. "So, Tori, why don't you just sit yourself down and let me hear what you have to say."

"Not here," Tati said. "Can we go someplace more, well, private?"

"Sure. Let's go to my office."

Being escorted through a crowded police precinct by a homicide detective reminded Tati of being ten years old and standing on the high dive at the water park, looking down and cowering, while feeling the pressure of everybody behind her getting impatient for her to jump. She felt like she couldn't go through with it.

"In here," Detective Witt said.

When Detective Witt closed the door behind them, Tati felt trapped. The office looked like an ornery child's bedroom after a tantrum. Piled on every horizontal surface were papers, binders, envelopes, calendars, construction paper, Post-it pads, poorly folded maps, mug shots, wanted notices, missing-person flyers, paper airplanes, and an in-basket containing everything from a filled-in March Madness bracket to the menu from the Golden Phoenix Buffet. The out-basket was empty save for a half-finished carton of carryout fried rice. A miniature backboard with basketball hoop was mounted on the rim of a trash can, and crumbled balls of paper littered the floor around it. Crushed cans of Red Bull overflowed from the recycling bin. The floor was sticky under the soles of her shoes.

Amid this hoard, occupying an entire wall behind the detective's desk, Huck's picture hung in the center of an immense corkboard, with strings connecting his image to newspaper clippings, crime-scene photos, handwritten notes ending in question marks, and, most disconcerting of all, photos of Huck's friends and colleagues, including herself. The picture of her wasn't particularly flattering—it looked like she'd been crying. Beneath it, the detective had written in marker on masking tape, "What did she know?"

Detective Witt removed a pizza box from the chair across from her desk. "Take a seat."

So far, this had gone pretty much the way Huck had predicted. Still, Tati was so nervous she felt cramps in her intestines. She reminded herself that she did this for Huck.

Tati put the file folder she carried with her onto the table. She then swallowed a mouthful of dry air and asked, "Could you please get me a glass of water?"

"Sure thing, sweetheart," Detective Witt said. "Make yourself comfortable. I'll be right back."

As soon as the detective rounded the corner, Tati took her cell out of her purse and started taking pictures. She took a photo of the crazy board. She rifled through stacks of paper and took photos of their contents as fast as she could. She clicked the mouse on the detective's desk computer, which opened her Twitter account, and took a picture of that. Finally, Tati opened the desk drawer—funny, she expected to find a bottle hidden there; isn't that how cops rolled? Instead, beneath loose files, envelopes, and spiral notebooks, there were cheap paperback novels crammed into the bottom of the drawer. In any event, she snapped several more photos. She finished and returned to her seat a second before the detective returned with a bottle of mineral water.

"How's this?" she asked.

"Good." Tati took the bottle and looked around for a place to put it, before finally sticking it between her legs.

"Aren't you going to drink?"

"Yeah, yeah, yeah. I, uh, forgot." Tati twisted the cap but couldn't get it open.

"Let me," the detective offered, then removed the cap with a half turn of her wrist. She handed the bottle back to Tati and said, "Don't be nervous."

Don't be nervous?!? Sure. Nothing to be nervous about. She was only stealing from and providing false witness to the police on behalf of an alleged felon. No problem.

"Will you be okay?"

"Uh huh. I think so, yeah."

"You can drink now."

Tati looked between her legs for the bottle, then remembered she had it in her hand. She gulped a mouthful, then coughed. "Sorry." She wiped her mouth with her arm.

"Don't mention it," Detective Witt said. "Are you ready to talk?"

"Talk about what?"

"About why you came to see me today."

Don't blow it, Tati scolded herself. "Yes. I'll talk."

"Do you mind if I record this?" Detective Witt asked.

Tati nodded.

"First, how do you know Mr. Carp."

"I met him at Drip 'n' Donuts."

"Are you in a relationship with him?"

"We're not related, if that's what you mean."

"No. Are you involved with him?"

"Involved?"

"I mean romantically. Is the nature of your relationship *intimate*?"

Intimate? Huck had told her the detective would ask how she knew him; she had prepared to say they were friends and leave it at that. But being asked about *intimacy* was something she hadn't considered. She liked that idea and paused to wonder if it might in some respects be true, at least a little bit. This emboldened her.

"Oh, you mean have we hooked up? Yeah. Once or twice. But I'm done with that now."

"Why so?"

"Duh. He's a murderer."

"All men are pigs." Detective Witt leaned across the desk to take Tati's hands in hers. "He can't hurt you anymore."

You're what scares me, Tati thought. "That's why I broke up with him."

"So, you believe he killed Adam Erb?"

"Why else would you have arrested him?"

Detective Witt blinked slowly, savoring such unquestioning deferral to authority.

Tati continued, "He hated Adam Erb. He admitted that much to me. I asked him why. He didn't answer in words. Instead, he showed me this."

She took the file folder she'd brought and held it so that Detective Witt could read the label, on which was written in Huck's handwriting, ERBonomics. The detective licked her lips when she accepted it. Huck had instructed Tati to watch her reaction when she opened the file. To Tati, she looked clueless, kind of stupid.

Detective Witt flipped through several articles stapled together. "What's this?" she asked, then read aloud the titles of several of them: "'Reflexive Control Theory and the Efficacy of Affective Forecasting;' 'A Grounded Theory Toward an Oppositional Culture of Financial Altruism;' 'Competitive Pro-Social Motivation and Pseudo-Altruistic Models of Capitalism;' 'A Multivariate Typology of Class Warfare Based upon Nonreciprocal Behaviors.'"

Tati shrugged. "It's all Greek to me. I thought you'd understand what it means."

Detective Witt closed the folder and pinched her eyes. "I need for somebody in the research department to look this over. We found thousands of articles like these on his computer. But if he gave you these in particular, maybe there's a clue in them, somewhere."

"I think so," Tati said. "I really do."

"If that's all, then, I thank you for bringing this to my attention."

Tati stood to leave. "It's too bad he's a bloodthirsty killer," she remarked. "Because I liked him."

The detective led her to the door. "Alas, men," she said. "They're all rank, nasty bastards. Am I right?"

"Amen to that," Tati said.

Detective Witt watched Tati until she left the precinct. Then she grabbed her coat, gun, and flak jacket, and she exited via the back door to avoid passing by the captain's office. Hopping into her Land Rover, she drove while listening to classic country music on the radio. She sang along with songs about broken hearts, drunken brawls, loving mothers, dead dogs, and old-time religion. Some twenty miles into her trip, she turned the radio off when "Happiest Girl in the Whole USA" played. That was about the last song in the entire canon of country music that she wanted to hear. "Skipitty doo dah my ass," she grumbled.

The unmarked and circuitous two-lane roads of rural Knox County were a perfect place for a criminal to hide out. Fortunately, the signal on Huck's ankle monitor led her directly to the Carp family farm. It was already dark when she arrived, and the Land Rover triggered a motion detector on a spotlight when she turned onto the dirt driveway. She chuckled when she passed the sign that said, "Property protected by Smith & Wesson."

A dark figure peeked between drawn curtains in an upstairs window. Seconds later, two shadows looked out the living room window. Detective Witt parked by the barn. Even from inside the car, with the heater blowing, she could hear a hog wail, "Ggggyyyyuuuukkkk, quuuurt, quuuurt," as if to sound an alarm.

Huck took one step outside and tapped his foot, while a porch swing next to him groaned in the cold breeze. Detective Witt remained in the idling vehicle, fingers fused into the steering wheel. For several seconds they faced each other across the yard, like gunslingers staring down each other.

Finally, the detective slammed the heel of her palm against the Land Rover's horn and held it there. Huck shuffled forward, not in any hurry. When he presented himself at the driver's side window, she yelled "Get in, shithead" through the glass.

Huck rounded the vehicle and entered the passenger side, emitting a heavy breath and a cloud of steam. "We don't get many visitors here after dark. You're lucky my mother didn't shoot."

"A woman after my own heart," the detective replied.

"So, what are you doing here?" Huck asked. "Are they dropping the charges against me?"

Detective Witt admired his confidence, but not as much as she resented his cockiness. "When hell freezes over."

"Then we have nothing to say to each other," Huck remarked, reaching for the door handle.

Detective Witt flipped a switch that locked the passenger side door. Huck's shoulders stiffened when he heard the door's lock click.

"Hold your horses," the detective said. "I got something to say to you."

"This is an illegal detention," he protested.

"Listen, shithead. If I meant to detain you, I'd have already cuffed you and jammed you into the trunk. Normally, I wouldn't even waste my breath speaking to you. But since you insist on pretending like you're your own lawyer, you need to hear me out. It's in your client's — that is, *your* — best interest."

"Very well." Huck faced her, but his eyes drifted toward her gun. "I'm listening."

"The district attorney is chomping at the bit to prosecute. The case against you is overwhelming."

"You've got nothing but coincidence and hearsay."

"Every day I get more evidence. I found some interesting things on your computer. For example, there's a note in your research journal where you wrote Adam Erb is a 'rogue variable' that needs to be 'rejected.' It was dated the day before the murder."

Huck blinked slowly, as if irritated at having to explain. "That merely proves I'm a conscientious researcher."

"I say it proves premeditation and motive."

"Objection. Calls for speculation."

"Well, I also found another entry where you referred to Adam Erb as — and I quote — " Detective Witt chirruped in the voice of an adult teasing a child, "'*a cootie bug-nose dripper.*'"

"Uhhhh," Huck stammered. "That's just something my mother says. It means he's a persistent annoyance."

"It speaks to your delusional mental state."

"Your conclusions would never pass peer review."

"Yeah, but do you really think you'll get a jury of peers?" Detective Witt could tell by Huck's silence that remark touched a nerve. She shifted to a somber tone. "The DA is going to seek the death penalty."

"The death penalty is unjust, immoral, and unworthy of enlightened civilization!"

"Duh. That's why it's so popular in America." Detective Witt sliced her hand slowly across her throat, then resumed. "But maybe there's room for negotiation. If, for instance, you were to confess, right here and now, I might be able to persuade her to take the death penalty off the table. You might get life without parole, but that's better than no life at all."

"Never!"

"Set aside your righteous indignation long enough to think it over. A bright guy like you could do well in prison. You could become a jailhouse lawyer and spend the rest of your life filing frivolous lawsuits on behalf of hardened criminals.

"And you could continue doing research. Prison is a perfect laboratory for studying what's wrong with society. Think about the experiments you could design, the hypotheses you could test, and the discoveries you could make. Being a convicted felon might even help you get published. I imagine those liberal journals you read would love it.

"And you wouldn't even have to worry about paying off your student loans. It's better than getting a big fat research grant."

Sally offered a handshake, hoping to seal the deal.

Huck's eyes darted side to side, as if looking at both sides of her proposition. At length, he opened his hand, extended it toward her... but at the last moment he pulled back and folded all his fingers except the middle one.

"As my mother would say, *ppppfuck you*."

Detective Witt half smiled. Just as she thought—Professor Huck Carp may be well educated, but he was just as dumb and obstinate as any other dude. "Fine, then," she spat. "I was just trying to save the taxpayers some money. Personally, I'll be just as happy to see you fry." She flipped the switch to unlock the passenger side door. "Now get out."

As Huck walked back to the house, Detective Witt switched on the radio, then turned it up when she recognized the song. She sang out loud to "Blue Yodel No. 8."

Yodel-a-ee-he-he
He-he-he-he-he-he

CHAPTER 10

In the ongoing clash over the monetization of Adam Erb's soul, Ginny Campbell had yet another idea for defeating D'Nisha Glint. She stalked another exclusive. She left messages via text, email, and telephone. She knocked on the door, but got no answer. Still, to get an in-depth, no-holds-barred, hopefully kiss-and-tell interview with Barb Knoop, Ginny resolved to do whatever was necessary, even if she had to ambush her.

For six interminably boring hours, she'd sat in the front seat of her Nissan Cube, staking out Barb's apartment. Troll and all his equipment were pretzeled into the back. Ginny recognized by the grimace of distress on his face that, after several cups of coffee, he was bloated from holding back flatulence.

"Do you have any more donuts?" Ginny called back to Troll.

Early that morning, they'd stopped at the Drip 'n' Donuts drive-thru. Ginny had placed a single red rose upon the Erb memorial, while Troll had ordered a thermos full of black coffee and a mixed dozen donuts. These provisions served for breakfast and lunch; it was now getting on toward time for Ginny's mid-afternoon snack.

"There's just one left."

"Hand it over." When she looked in the bag, Ginny groaned. "That's it? One plain cake donut?"

"I didn't expect we'd be here so long, and I got hungry," Troll explained. "I'm a growing boy."

"Growing in all the wrong places."

Troll removed a white handkerchief from his pocket and waved it like a surrender flag. Ginny enjoyed bantering with him, so long as she always got in the last word.

The donut was spongy and tasteless, and when Ginny tried to swallow, her stomach pushed back. A clog coalesced in her throat. She flailed with her hands, grasping for the thermos, which she discovered was empty.

"Are you okay?" Troll asked.

In the suspended second that she felt the spasm rise into her throat, Ginny weighed her options for vomiting. Since she couldn't lower the window in time, her only choice short of hurling onto her lap was to regurgitate the masticated donut back into the bag from whence it had come. She buried her face into the open bag and let fly.

As if now excused to do so, Troll let rip a massive fart. Mephitic gasses permeated the air and burned their lungs.

"Seriously?" Ginny gagged.

"Sorry," Troll said.

Ginny held the bag over her face, preferring to breath the fumes of her own puke than the fallout from Troll's viscera. She rolled down the car's windows. Troll fanned the air with his handkerchief. Ginny felt the odor penetrate to her internal organs, in particular her bladder. Until that moment, she hadn't realized how badly she needed to piss. This was a hazard of doing a stakeout they never showed in detective movies.

"Maybe we should try later," Troll suggested.

When faced with any obstacle in the performance of her job, Ginny always asked herself, *What would D'Nisha do?* And then she did the opposite. Without a doubt, D'Nisha Glint would quit rather than persevere against boredom, nausea, and physical discomfiture in hope of getting a story. Ginny had the gumption of a genuine reporter, while D'Nisha was merely a bimbo who read from a teleprompter.

Ginny clenched her cheeks and grunted, "We're staying."

This rivalry between her and D'Nisha was just business. True, Ginny hated her guts and wouldn't weep a single tear if she suffered some non-lethal — but grossly disfiguring — accident. Without her looks, the bitch would be nothing. But it wasn't personal.

Ginny had to be smarter and work harder than D'Nisha to get ratings. The only standard of newsworthiness that mattered was whether a story captured the audience's attention. Good gossip never failed to attract viewers, and it proliferated without regard to its truth or utility. So, Ginny approached every story by wondering whether it would make people's tongues flap. That morning, Ginny's best idea for hijacking the public's awareness was to get an exclusive interview with the woman that everybody wanted to hear from — even if they didn't know it yet. Barb Knoop. An interview with Adam's star-crossed lover and future mother of a little Erb was a surefire ticket to the top of the ratings. Even better, D'Nisha Glint wouldn't have an answer for it.

Ginny readjusted the rearview mirror. Throughout the morning, she had fiddled with the mirror repeatedly, mostly out of boredom, but also because it enabled her to keep an eye on Troll. She felt funny having her back to him. She was surprised to see Troll looking back at her in the mirror.

"Down, boy," she said.

"I wasn't looking at you," he insisted.

"You'd better not be."

"I wasn't."

"Don't get any ideas."

"Don't worry. I like dudes."

Ginny felt strangely insulted by this disclosure. That was pertinent information he'd never imparted to her. It was embarrassing because she'd been absolutely positive he had the hots for her. If she'd known he was gay, she wouldn't have treated him so poorly.

Troll continued, "Adam Erb had lots of gay admirers."

"No!" Ginny snapped. Why did she feel defensive about that?

For the next several minutes, they ignored each other. Ginny couldn't banish the image of Adam Erb and Troll together in bed. She was about to throw in the towel and suggest they give up, when—

"Isn't that her?" Troll pointed at a woman approaching on the sidewalk.

It was! Ginny forgot all about sex. "Let's roll," she hollered, and hit the street running.

Barb Knoop wore a hood, dark glasses, and an ankle-length trench coat, but the distinctive hitch in her gait gave her away. She walked on her heels and sides, as if nursing inflamed bunions. When she saw Ginny coming, she started to run for it, but turned her ankle shortly after breaking into a jog.

Realizing that she had Barb cornered, Ginny approached in slow small steps.

"I got nothing to say to the press," Barb said.

"Fine. Let's talk as friends," Ginny replied.

"Friends?"

"I want to be your friend," Ginny assured her.

"I ain't got many friends these days." Barb removed her sunglasses and wiped her eyes with the back of her hand. "What the hell, then. Maybe I'll talk, but off the record, okay?"

Ginny reached one arm behind her back so Troll could witness her crossed fingers. "If that's how you want it."

Barb kicked a stone and watched it skip down the sewer. "I guess it's okay. Adam trusted you. Come along."

Barb's apartment was in a Lego-like complex off Innis Road, across abandoned railroad tracks from a drive-thru beverage dealership, where on a clear day you could hear customers hollering into the intercom to order cases of whatever beer was on sale. She lived on the third floor. There was no elevator, so they took the stairs. The mat outside of Barb's door read: Welcome—Unless You're the Police. Barb told them to make themselves at home, which to Troll meant looking in her refrigerator.

"Can I have a beer?" he asked.

Ginny glowered at him, but Barb said, "Help yourself to a PBR. And grab one for me too."

"Make that three," Ginny added. This was one of those times when drinking on the job was permissible in the service of journalism.

Barb moved a basket of laundry off an easy chair for Ginny to sit. She wrapped a shawl across her shoulders and pulled a rocker across the room, sitting so close to Ginny that when she rocked forward their noses were within a foot of each other's. Troll settled in a folding chair at the dining table. Ginny winked at Troll, who placed his camera on the tabletop; when Barb wasn't looking, he turned it on.

"How're you doing?" Ginny asked.

"I manage. Every day, I lay a flower at that memorial at Drip 'n' Donuts."

"I understand. Adam's death shocked all of us. But you had a special relationship with him, didn't you?"

"It was special to me. I think it was special to him, too. At least for a night."

"I'm sure it was. Adam was, deep down, a hopeless romantic."

"How would you know?" Barb snapped. She stopped rocking. "Did you screw him too?"

"Absolutely not! Our relationship was purely professional."

"Don't get snippy. I didn't mean nothing by asking. Besides, to tell the truth just between us girls" — Barb cupped her hand and whispered into Ginny's ear — "he was far from the best I've ever had."

Ginny felt her heart flutter. "Seriously?"

"Listen, I don't kid myself about Adam." Barb cracked her knuckles. "Maybe I'm just a sucker. But when he picked me out of all the women in Daisy Mae's and asked me to dance, it *did* make me feel special. And, well, he knocked me up, alright. I guess that definitely makes me more special than any others."

Ginny had heard a hundred versions of this story before; she knew Adam's modus operandi so well that listening to Barb was like binge-watching reruns — which made it inscrutable that the night would end with Barb's insemination. Adam used condoms fastidiously.

"So, he took you dancing?" she prodded.

"We only danced to one song, 'Boot Scootin' Boogie.' Then he told me I was beautiful. He told me he had his eye on me from the moment he first walked into the tavern. He asked my name, and I said Miss America. He thought that was funny, then asked me if I would 'do him the *honor*' of spending the night with him."

"That sounds very romantic."

"No, it sounds like bullshit. Trust me. I've heard every pickup line in the book. If he'd been anybody else, I'd have told him to not let the door hit his ass on the way out. But I thought to myself, this is Mr. Talking Truth himself, and that made me want to believe. Plus, I can't deny he's a stud. So, I said to myself, *Barb — you go for it.*"

Ginny offered a sympathetic nod, although she wanted to laugh. She knew, perhaps better than anybody, that Adam Erb's truth was whatever version of reality suited his desires. That whole business about "talking truth" was just his impeccably crafted schtick, saying what other people wanted to say and telling them what they wanted to hear. Few people saw through his faux sincerity because doubting him would have required them to doubt themselves.

"What happened next?" Ginny asked.

"We went to his limo. I was ready to get busy right away. But he didn't seem in any hurry. He said he wanted to take me home. That sounded good to me. On the way, he gave me some papers to sign."

"Papers?"

"A form that said I consented to sexual activity with him. Another certifying that to my knowledge I ain't got no communicable diseases. And another swearing me to confidentiality. He promised me this was all just a formality upon advice from his legal counsel. I wasn't thrilled about it—kind of ruined the mood, y'know—but I figured that, for a millionaire, this was like foreplay."

"So, you signed them?"

"Well it wasn't like I was going to ask him to wait until I had my lawyer look them over, so, yeah, I signed them. Now, I'm glad that I did. Look...."

Barb took her cell phone from her back pocket and scrolled through photos until she found what she was looking for, then showed it to Ginny. She'd made copies of all the legal forms. Her name was signed with valentine hearts for the *o*'s in Knoop.

"I took this photo when he wasn't looking, so I'd have *proof*."

Barb broke into a grin. Ginny reciprocated with a chuckle. Then they both buckled over laughing, while Troll took the opportunity to fetch another beer.

After a few seconds, Barb regained her composure and resumed her story. "When we got to his mansion, he took me into his bedroom, gave me a slinky little teddy, and asked me to put it on. He then told me to wait, while he disappeared into to the bathroom for what seemed like forever. When he finally came back, he was butt naked and harder than a titanium battering ram wrapped in steel reinforced concrete."

Ginny winked. "I get the picture."

"Wham bam boom." Barb smacked her fists together. "When we finished, he rolled over and fell asleep. But he was still hard, even while snoring and out like a light. I thought that was weird until...." Barb averted her eyes and gnawed on her lower lip.

"Until what?"

"After he'd fallen asleep, I went into the bathroom to splash myself off. That's when I saw a bottle of Viagra on a shelf behind the sink. All of a sudden I understood how he got so much staying power. He must've dosed himself up good."

"I see. It's a medical condition with some men." Ginny couldn't believe she was making excuses for Adam Erb. If he wasn't dead, he'd owe her big time. Actually, he owed her anyway.

"I don't take it personal. He was nice to me the next morning, gave me breakfast, took me home in his limo. I got no complaints. At first, I couldn't help but wonder how I measured up compared to his other ladies. He was Adam Erb, after all, and he'd been with lots of beautiful women. I wondered if he'd even remember me. I gave him my phone number and hoped he would call. He never did."

Barb pressed both hands against her breast, as if steadying her heart. "Then I listened to his very last podcast. At the end he said something that, I swear, he meant just for me, like he was telling me he loved me. That's what made me feel special. If he hadn't died, I think that, maybe, he'd have come back for me."

"Wow. What did he say?"

"I downloaded the podcast so I could listen again and again. Sit tight and I'll play it for you."

Barb had an app linked to Adam Erb's homepage on her cell phone. She opened it and scrolled through several screens before landing on the download for February 12. She fast-forwarded through Adam's rant about crime in the city, his screed against the cowardly mayor, his diatribe against the liberal media, and his harangue about the waste of taxpayers' money on public transportation, until reaching minute twenty-nine of his half-hour podcast, then she pressed play and turned up the volume.

Adam spoke: "Finally, in conclusion, I want to remind my listeners that this is Valentine's Day weekend. Remember to do right by the one you love—or the *ones* you love. Ha. Just kidding. As you know, I love love—and even better if it's with somebody you like. Ha. Just kidding, again. But seriously—"

Adam sniffed, cleared his throat.

"I do believe in true love, heart to heart and soul to soul. In fact, there's a special woman out there. She's somebody who's never weak, but always strong, who'll protect me and defend me whether I'm right or wrong. She's there for me behind each and every door. She knows who she is, so I'll just call her *Miss America*."

Barb paused the audio, reversed it, and played it once again. Upon finishing, she lifted the cell phone to her lips and kissed the screen.

"When I heard Adam say those words, I broke down blubbering, 'cause I knew he was talking about me. You heard it, right?"

"Right," Ginny said, even though she didn't believe it.

Out of the corner of her eye, she watched Troll stick a finger in his mouth and pantomime gagging. Ginny scolded him by making a slashing gesture across her throat. Fortunately, Barb gazed dreamily toward the ceiling and missed seeing his shenanigans.

"It's as if he knew, somehow, that I carried his baby," Barb supposed.

"Right," was all Ginny could say.

Barb continued by telling of strange coincidences she had recently experienced, which she took as Adam communicating with her from the other side—like her cell phone suddenly playing "Sugarfoot Rag" for no reason, and hearing his voice call her name over the intercom at Kmart. Ginny agreed that those were odd occurrences indeed. Then she coughed.

On cue, Troll said, "Hey, boss. You're gonna be late for that meeting."

"Oh shoot," Ginny cried. "Time has sped by. I must go. But thank you so much, Barb."

"You sure you have to leave? I got some Oreo cookies."

Troll hesitated, but Ginny kicked him in the shins. She apologized, "So sorry. But the news waits for nobody."

As soon as they were outside, Ginny broke into gales of laughter. "I hope you got all of that, because every word of it is pure gold."

"Every batshit crazy word of it. But—" Troll cleared his throat. "Do you really think we ought to use it? She thought she was talking off the record. You even said you were her friend."

"Snap out of it!" Ginny screeched and stomped on his foot. "I've gone too far to stop now. Of course I'm going to use it!"

She offered Troll a high five. He batted his hand against hers, then wiped his palm on his trousers.

"You're the boss," Troll said.

"Damn right! I only wish I could see the expression on D'Nisha Glint's face when we broadcast it."

The gentle newsroom ambiance of pattering fingertips upon keyboards, papers being crumpled and tossed into trash cans, and the susurrations of people thinking out loud seemed entirely too normal to D'Nisha. The ill-suited quietude triggered an explosion like multiple aneurysms in her head. She jumped onto her desk and shrieked, "NOOOMOTHERFUCKINGWAAAAY!!!!!"

The weatherwoman ducked and covered. A news writer fled via the fire exit. Several crew members playing cards in the break room closed the door and blocked it with a chair. The camera dude, who'd been wearing noise-canceling headphones while listening to Slayer, removed them and called out, "What's the deal, D'Nisha?"

D'Nisha hurled her Ohio State Fair Butter Queen trophy out the door of her office. The camera dude peeked around the door, arms raised and hands open. "You okay in there?"

"NOIAMNOTFUCKINGOKAY," D'Nisha raged.

She stood on top of her desk, brandishing a letter opener in one hand and an open stapler in the other. Her coiffed hair had broken out into its natural corkscrew afro, exposing stark white roots. If her eyes opened any wider, they'd have met in the middle. She panted like a predator just outrun by its prey.

Camera dude slowly reached into a lower drawer on her desk and took out a pillbox. "Have a Zantac?" He shook the bottle.

"Gimme that!" D'Nisha growled. She shook ten onto her palm and slapped them down her throat, then closed her eyes, waiting for them to take effect.

The camera dude granted her a moment before asking, "Having a bad day?"

"It's that gangrenous cunt, Ginny Campbell," D'Nisha said. "She got an interview with Adam Erb's bitch."

"Which one?"

"The one that claims to be pregnant with his demon seed," she said. "The same one that turned me down for an interview — not once, not twice, but *three times*. How dare she, that pus-sucking whore!"

"Ouch,"camera dude said.

"That does it. No more Ms. Nicey Nice," she said. "I'm going to unleash an Internet bomb that will blow Ginny Campbell's ass from cheeks to colon."

"That's harsh."

"I thought once Adam Erb was dead that'd be the end of him. Rest in peace and good riddance. I would have kept his secrets zipped. I hated him, but I still owed him. Now, thanks to Miss Ginny 'the Donkey Slut' Campbell, there are seriously bodacious ratings at stake. I can't let this aggression go unanswered."

D'Nisha pulled a chair up in front of her laptop. She opened a browser to the Erb Is a Dick web page, then logged on as Admin.

"Are you the Erb Is a Dick webmaster?" camera dude asked.

"For the most part this site needs very little maintenance," D'Nisha said, clicking on the Edit Content button. "But, yeah, I created the page. At the time, I was really pissed at him. Once I put it up, I couldn't take it down. I had no idea that Adam had so many haters. They needed a place to blow off steam."

D'Nisha opened a second window on her screen; an extensive directory filled it, containing multitudinous emails, organized chronologically as far back as ten years, all with the same author: Adam Erb. D'Nisha scrolled through them like shuffling cards.

"Where did you get all of those emails from Erb?" the camera dude asked.

"I have sources," D'Nisha said dismissively. "There are probably thousands of them—on every subject from stock futures to gun rights, from point spreads to prostate massages, sent to everybody from his agent to his podiatrist, from his dry cleaner to his chauffeur, and to scores upon scores of women. At first I didn't intend to use this information. But things have changed."

"How so?" camera dude asked.

In D'Nisha's mind, two things had changed. First, she had purged the Erb omnibus of every single email in which she was named. She had no desire to share those on the Internet. The second thing that changed she summed up as, "Ginny started this war! But I'll end it!"

D'Nisha pressed Select All and labeled everything in the directory with a new hashtag, #OvERBearing.

"Are you really going to...?"

"Watch this," she said, and with a flourish forwarded every one of those emails to the thousands of contacts from the Erb Is a Dick website and Facebook page. As she'd anticipated, this triggered a domino effect from those contacts to their contacts, and to countless others, across every social media account in their collective repertoire. Almost immediately, her computer started pinging like popcorn popping to alert her to incoming mail.

"Ha!" D'Nisha cackled, rubbing her hands together. "Let Ginny Campbell choke on *that*."

CHAPTER 11

"Good mornin', captain," Detective Sally Witt said when the captain poked his nose through the crack she'd left open on her office door.

"What'd you do?" he asked.

Sally had rearranged her office since the captain's last trespass. Now when she sat behind the desk, she faced the door, with her back to the crazy board on the wall. Even though the captain could not see her computer monitor, she minimized the web page on its screen.

"Just a little spring cleaning," she answered.

"I don't like it." The captain bent over her desk and leaned forward on his knuckles. "What's the matter? Did you have a rough night?"

"No," she answered. She'd actually had a good night. For the first time in days, she'd gone home, made some hot buttered rum, and curled up with her favorite reading material.

"Go splash some water in your face," the captain told her. "You look like shit on spaghetti."

Sally saluted. "Aye, aye, captain." Anything to get rid of him.

When the captain left, Sally reopened her browser to the Erb Is a Dick web page. New comments came in as fast as tumblers on a slot machine, each with the same hashtag, #OvERBearing. Each new posting contained fragments of or comments on emails written by Adam Erb, on an encyclopedia's worth of subjects. There was enough raw material in this anthology to keep a biographer or a psychoanalyst occupied for decades. More germane, however, was that this was all potential evidence that Sally had to process.

She looked forward to it. She never got bored with #MemERBilia.

Suddenly, her computer screen blinked System Error, then everything went blank, leaving her cursor stranded immobile in the middle of the screen. She tried Ctrl+Alt+Del, but the computer monitor remained suffused with a gray digital fog.

"Goddamnit," she muttered. "Just when I was getting to a juicy part."

"Pssst," Chavonne breathed into Tati's ear. Startled, Tati swallowed her chewing gum. Chavonne kept walking toward her office. She peeked back at Tati and jogged her head in a *follow me* gesture.

Tati counted to ten before stepping away from her workstation. "I'm taking my break," she told her co-workers. They muttered "yeah" and "sure," but paid no attention as she walked past the break room and slipped around the corner into Chavonne's office and gently closed the door behind her.

"Do you have some news about the case?" she asked hopefully.

Chavonne sat at her desk in front of the computer. "Grab a chair," she said. "Come take a look at this."

Tati looked over Chavonne's shoulder as she clicked on a link in her favorites bar, and the word Welcome rippled in a banner across the top of her monitor. Beneath the banner was the SECS logo: a leather belt with a chain mesh genital harness and a heart-shaped lock and key. Chavonne clicked on it.

"I passed," Chavonne said. "I'm a celibate."

A pair of ruffled theater curtains opened, revealing an empty stage. Rolling words in script serif font materialized against an eggshell-white background.

Congratulations. Upon careful review, I have determined that you are eligible to join our elite community. I am proud to welcome you to the Society of Enlightened Celibate Savants.

"I'm now what yo' call officially *SECSY.*" Chavonne gave herself a thumbs up.

Tati patted her on the back. "Good for you. That was quick."

"I guess I qualify on account of my shitty love life. It's a club of nuns, eunuchs, losers, incels, and old maids. I'll fit right in."

"Don't forget—you're only doing this for Huck's sake," Tati reminded her.

The words faded from the screen and new text emerged. Tati and Chavonne read silently together.

We are a nonprofit member-support and social-advocacy organization that exists to promote the benefits of secular celibacy. Our society charges no dues. We are entirely self-supporting through the contributions of volunteers and benefactors. Membership entitles you to free access of the full range of our services and resources.

"This sounds kinda sketchy," Chavonne remarked. "Ain't nothing free, not even if it's something that most people don't want. There's got to be some catch."

"Don't give them your Social Security number," Tati cautioned her.

Again, the screen went blank and was refreshed with new text.

> *The only requirement to join our society is that you commit to the celibate lifestyle. This is not a step to take lightly. Many have failed to meet this obligation, and as a consequence have been banished from our community. However, if you believe in the purity and righteousness of our cause, then all you must do to finalize your commitment is to read the* Celibacy Manifesto *and click to agree with it.*

"What the fuck is a manifesto?" Chavonne asked. "Sounds like something on the menu of an Italian restaurant."

"I think it's something like the Pledge of Allegiance," Tati conjectured.

"Well, shit, if that's true, I ain't worried, 'cuz I've done said the Pledge of Allegiance a million times in school, and I never knew what it meant."

A blank sheet of parchment paper appeared on the screen, and a quill pen wrote the following:

The Celibacy Manifesto
Whereas we recognize that countless hearts have been broken, fortunes squandered, empires lost, and lives destroyed by carnal lust,

And whereas throughout history deadly and incapacitating diseases have spread like plagues through infected acts of profligate passions and the exchange of tainted bodily fluids,

And whereas unbridled libido afflicts not only the body but also assaults the cognitive and emotional fitness of its victims through jealousy, obsession, depression, paranoia, and other manifestations of an enfeebled mind,

Therefore, we, the members of the Society of Enlightened Celibate Savants, recognize the ruinous effects of sexual activity upon the individual and society,

And while we acknowledge that breeders serve a vital societal function – i.e., the propagation of our species – we nevertheless hold that the celibate lifestyle is more conducive to maximizing human potential.

Therefore, we, the members of the Society of Enlightened Celibate Savants, believe and vouchsafe the following principles:

1. Sex is dangerous.

2. Those who practice sex lie about it.

3. Those who practice sex cannot be trusted to make wise decisions.

4. Celibacy is a more evolved way of living, which raises human beings above mere beasts.

5. Abstinence from sexual activity improves health.

6. Abstinence from sexual activity clarifies the body, soul, and mind.

7. Abstinence from sexual activity removes flaws, corrects defects, and purges wickedness.

8. Abstinence from sexual activity improves relationships by building trust, honesty, patience, and acceptance.

9. Abstinence from sexual activity frees the soul.

And...

10. Only through abstinence from sexual activity is it possible to achieve total self-actualization.

Be it thus resolved that on the 28th day of the month of February, 2017, I, Chavonne Hayes pledge myself to these principles and accept membership in the Society of Enlightened Celibate Savants, with all of the honors and obligations that entails.

Upon completing the manifesto, the quill pen vanished from the page. In its place at the bottom of the page there appeared an image of a fat, obviously-phallic cigar (at least it was obvious to Tati), with a thick band wrapped around its shaft. It read, Click Here to Accept.

Tati finished reading the document sooner than Chavonne, then watched her trace the text with her finger and mouth the words silently, the better to let them sink in. Chavonne reached the bottom of the page and hovered the cursor over the cigar band, her finger twitching above the left-click button on her mouse. Her eyes flitted back and forth in rapid thought.

"This here looks like some kind of a legal contract," Chavonne remarked at length.

"Listen, you don't have to go through with this. I think you already got enough information. Let me talk about it to Huck first."

But before Tati finished speaking, whether on purpose or by some involuntary twitch, Chavonne clicked on the cigar band. A flame ignited the tip of the cigar, and it glowed hot red, as if somebody stoked it. Smoke rings in the shape of valentine hearts rose on the page.

"Too late," Chavonne said. "What's the worst that could happen?"

Tati envisioned midnight bed checks, photo surveillance, and/or surgical castration, but she refrained from citing those for Chavonne's further consideration.

While the cigar continued burning, a window labeled Resources for a Joyous Celibacy popped up, beneath which were links to all sorts of diversions and amenities, like Games, Recipes, Reading List, Just for Laughs, and Thought for the Day. Simultaneously, a sidebar appeared on the right side of the screen, containing links to Member Services, including My Profile, Our Products, My Shopping Cart, Technical Support, and Dating Services.

"Dating services?" Tati wondered. "I mean, what do they do on a date?"

"Let's find out." Chavonne clicked on that link.

A little black book flew in from the bottom of the screen. It opened to a table of contents: Straight Men, Straight Women, Gay, Lesbian, Bisexual Men, Bisexual Women, Polyamorous, and Other. Each category linked to celibates of the appropriate sexual orientation who were "eager to make a love connection."

"I never would've guessed that so many people in Columbus have sworn off sex," Tati remarked, then further wondered, "What the hell do they do with all their extra time?"

Chavonne dismissed Tati's question by saying, "I spent mo' time clipping my toenails last year than having sex."

She then started binge clicking, opening window after window of eligible bachelors seeking a celibate partner. "Hot damn." She stopped for one jacked brother wearing a tangle of silver and gold necklaces and no shirt; he sat on the hood of a tricked-out pink Buick Riviera. "Me oh my oh, that's some mess of man flesh."

"Yeah, but what good is it if he doesn't do the horizontal tango?" Tati asked.

"Well, listen here to this..." Chavonne paraphrased from his personality statement, "...he likes doing yoga, cooking fancy dinners and serving them by candlelight, doing the woah dance at the Electric Company, and bingeing Denzel Washington movies in bed. Damn, I like him already."

"Okay. I get it, up to a point," Tati said. "But let's say you're in bed with him watching Denzel cozy up with Paula Patton. Ain't that going to make you start tingling around your lady parts, no matter how so-called celibate you'd be?"

Chavonne reflected upon that scenario. "Maybe we'd go to the Electric Company and do the woah instead."

Tati felt a chuckle start deep in her belly and rise to the back of her throat, but she held it back until Chavonne laughed first, which was a relief. She wasn't sure if being celibate meant you couldn't laugh, too.

Chavonne kept clicking on links as fast as if the mouse tickled the palm of her hand. "Let's take a look at the competition." She opened the little black book to where Straight Women were listed. There was a scrolling A–Z bar down the side of the page. Chavonne spun the wheel on the mouse and watched as names whirled by.

"*¡Madre de Dios!*" Tati said in disbelief. "There're enough lady celibates listed here to fill up their own zip code."

"Abigail, Acacia, Addison, Alisha, Amelia... Damn, I ain't even got to the *B*s yet."

Tati pointed to a Search box at the top. "Can I check something?"

Chavonne scooted aside to allow Tati to use the keyboard. She entered the name Val Vargas, but it came back with zero matches.

"That's weird," Tati said. She tried again—same result.

"Yo' must not know how it works."

"Or maybe she's listed in another category? Maybe she's bi?"

Tati selected a global search function and typed in Val, followed by a wild card to retrieve all possible variations of her surname. When she pressed Enter, a System Error message appeared, then the monitor faded to black, the keyboard locked up, and even the beach ball spinning in the corner of the screen froze.

"I didn't do nothing wrong, did I?" Tati wondered.

"I don't think so," Chavonne said, "because my cell phone went blank too."

D'Nisha couldn't believe it. Apparently, she had crashed the Internet. According to information from her usually reliable tipsters, the Net was down across all of

Columbus and its suburbs, except for Obetz, where nobody used the Internet anyway. It couldn't have been mere coincidence that this plague upon hyperspace struck within just minutes after she jettisoned a colossal trove of Adam Erb's emails bearing the hashtag #OvERBearing into social media. Of course, she couldn't prove she'd personally started the fatal chain reaction, but she would happily take credit for creating the trend to end all trends. She had out-Erbed Adam.

D'Nisha dashed out of her office and shouted, "Listen up!" into the WCBN newsroom.

It was midmorning, so most of the crew were on their coffee breaks. The weatherwoman had just returned from Drip 'n' Donuts with a box of assorted donuts, which was open on the conference table for friends and colleagues to share.

D'Nisha shouted, "Stop whatever you're doing. Now!"

Everybody stopped chewing.

"What the fuck does Princess D'Nisha want now?" the weatherwoman griped to the handful of others sitting around the table with her.

"I heard that," D'Nisha snapped. It was the first time she'd heard anybody refer to her as Princess D'Nisha. She liked it. "I have breaking news," she continued. "Have any of you tried to connect to the Internet recently?"

They answered with shrugs and blank expressions.

"You can't. Because it crashed. Parts of five counties, maybe more, went black suddenly, just like that." She snapped her fingers. "This is huge news. Gigantic news. So I'm going to break the story. All of you, get to your stations. I'm cutting into regular programming to deliver a special report."

"Are you seriously going to preempt Regis and Kelly?" camera dude asked.

"Am I serious!?!" D'Nisha picked up a jelly donut and tossed it at him like a Frisbee.

"Ouch," he complained.

"Are you okay, Abelard?" The weatherwoman asked him.

Abelard? What kind of a name was that? D'Nisha thought.

"I'm fine, Dagmar," the camera dude said.

Dagmar? Who are these people? Oh, never mind....

"This is a massive story," D'Nisha cried. "And it's all mine. So, get ready people. I'm going live in sixty seconds!"

D'Nisha squared herself in front of the news desk, smoothed her hair, and started counting backwards from sixty, while the news crew scrambled to execute her commands. At five, she counted the seconds out loud, "Five, four, three, two, one."

She pointed at camera dude—er, Abelard—and he returned a thumbs up.

"Good morning, Columbus, this is D'Nisha Glint, and I interrupt our regular program with an extra special report...."

Val dumped a bag of garlic- and parmesan-flavored microwave popcorn into a bowl, poured a glass of Red Bull with a shot of vodka, plunged into her easy chair, and said to Minou, "This is going to be so cool."

The cat brushed against Val's ankles and purred. She tossed it a nugget of popcorn, which it batted around like a toy.

When D'Nisha Glint unleashed the Erb email dump that morning, people's insanely exuberant reactions inundated social media throughout central Ohio, to the near exclusion of any other topic. In the first wave, a deluge of network traffic bearing the hashtag #OvERBearing cascaded downstream into the accounts of legions of end users logging on for the first time that morning. The second wave, which still hadn't crested, consisted of hundreds of thousands of individual responses and reactions bearing their own hashtags. Plotted with time on the y axis and volume on the x axis, the daily track looked like a lazy baseline interrupted by a sudden massive heart attack at the moment the dump landed in people's in-baskets, at which point the Internet hemorrhaged. The aggregate postings proliferated across multiple media and platforms. The result was that demand exceeded the network's bandwidth, like a fire hose shooting into a funnel.

This was a genuine five-alarm Internet emergency. Val had believed that only events the magnitude of a royal wedding, a world cup soccer victory, or naked photos of a celebrity could trigger such a frenzy. It defied all odds that anything coming out of little old Columbus might generate that kind of pandemonium. Yet it was happening, right before her very eyes. It was almost the most beautiful thing she had ever seen.

This wasn't about Adam Erb anymore. The media had become the message. Nobody could remain neutral. In life, Adam was a patrician turned playboy turned pundit turned predator turned pontificator. It was possible to love or hate him, but many people did not care about him one way or the other. In death, though, he became a meme, an icon, a cause, a champion, an antihero, an urban legend, and a virus. His online reincarnation was a many-faced avatar with manifestations in every niche and fissure of the Internet. An Erb hashtag bypassed the brain centers for rational thought and lodged directly in the hypothalamus, infecting its host with an emotional reaction that expressed itself in an immense social media seizure. Its only limit was the carrying capacity of the Internet itself.

Val knew what she had to do. She'd rigged the master control panel on her network hub with a red button. To prevent herself from pressing it by mistake, she'd covered the button with duct tape, on which she wrote in thick Sharpie, Don't! Val stood behind the desk and looked down at the red button with awe, humility, and reverence. She extended her index finger in front of her face. It wasn't a pretty digit—not shapely like a hand model's, strong like a masseuse's, or elegant like a pianist's. Then it occurred to her that it looked like God's crooked finger in Michelangelo's *Creation of Adam*. That seemed apropos.

She peeled the duct tape away from the red button. Uncovered, it looked like just another switch on her console, and yet she knew pressing it would initiate online reverberations that would change the world—or if not the *whole* world, at least Columbus—forever. She could not make the decision to press it lightly. Was she worthy? She could leave it alone and just walk away; some things were better left unknown.

But that wouldn't be any fun. She stiffened her finger directly above the red button and brought it straight down, as if poking somebody in the eye.

In so doing, Val dispatched every single one of that morning's innumerable posts in all her social media accounts to every single one of her followers. Her name was attached to millions of newly-birthed memetic contributions to the networked universe.

The giant screen blinked once, but picked right up tallying activity, like returning after a short time out. No alarm went off. To all appearances, nothing changed. Doubts assailed Val. Maybe her program was flawed. Or maybe she wasn't as powerful an influencer as she'd believed.

Val pressed the button again, as if re-ringing an unanswered doorbell. Still nothing.

"Banana shenanigans!" she blurted. "This can't be right."

Val walked to the window and tossed aside the curtains. She squinted against the unexpected sunshine and visored her eyes with her hand. All along the span of the Scioto Mile, she saw the normal pedestrian bustle of people intent on getting somewhere. Kids played. Bicyclists chugged along. Teenagers clustered together to vape. It all looked discouragingly typical.

Then Val watched one businesswoman with her nose in her cell phone stop in her tracks. Next, a man walking his dog skidded to a halt and stared at his phone. A teenage girl swiped her finger across the screen of her cell repeatedly, with increasing dismay and frustration. Within seconds, nearly everybody along the riverfront was fiddling with their cell phones. And when they realized that the same malfunction had affected each other's phones, somebody screamed, and the bemused masses ran howling for sanctuary, as if fearing a terrorist attack.

Val's own cell phone started vibrating and became hot to the touch. She wrapped her palm in a handkerchief to remove it from her pocket, then laid it flat and faceup on the windowsill. Characters whizzed across its screen like subatomic particles accelerating toward an explosive collision. Val tried to pause the text, but none of her commands functioned. Furthermore, the same breakneck messaging flashed across every monitor of every computer in Val's entire network. Helpless but to watch, she pried her eyelids open with her fingers so she wouldn't blink and miss something. Her senses spun.

Just as Val was about to faint, the runaway text slammed against an unmovable barrier, and a coruscation of pixels showered across every screen in her domain. Images that flashed and dazzled on one screen spilled onto the next, and the next, around the room in a continuous matrix of electronic fireworks. As the sparks settled onto the bottoms of so many screens, a sliver of brilliant white light burst across Val's giant monitor, and all the data vanished in a blink. The Internet succumbed.

"Cheez Whiz!" she shouted, pumping her fist.

Val wasn't sure exactly what happened, but she believed that it was unlike anything that had ever happened before. This was uncharted territory, a Nobel-caliber discovery. This was a higher spiritual realm of being, the quantum Internet, where trends never died. In this dimension, memes were immortal and trends paid it forward for all of eternity. She named her discovery the "Vargas Zone," a habitable region for a new digital species.

"I told you this was going to be cool," she gloated to Minou.

But it wasn't enough to have discovered the Vargas Zone. She needed to document it, develop a model, study its implications for humanity, and report back to the rest of civilization.

Val was glad she had the foresight to keep a land line in her condominium. She hadn't used that phone in — well, she'd never used that phone before. There was a delicious irony to using twentieth century technology to break the news of an advanced cybernetic breakthrough. She lifted the receiver and tingled upon hearing the dial tone. It sounded like her mantra. She dialed.

"Hello?" The voice on the other end of the line sounded puzzled.

"Huck! It's you!" Val cheered. "Wait until I tell you what I just did."

CHAPTER 12

Tati skipped her afternoon lecture in deviant sociology to fret at home, waiting for the phone to ring. Huck was overdue to call her. The last time they spoke, he swore he would call back in one week. That was eight days ago.

After her last shift at Drip 'n' Donuts, she'd brought home a mixed-dozen day-old donuts, which she meant to share with the whole family. Instead, she stashed them for herself, and all night long she fussed, paced, talked to herself, and gobbled donuts. By morning, she'd eaten eleven of them, leaving only one stale apple fritter. She felt bloated, and her tongue tasted like a slick coating of grape jelly, chocolate icing, and powdered sugar. Still, the fritter beckoned her, its sugary glaze catching flashes of morning sunlight, and its apple chunks floating in pinwheels of cinnamon. She felt beyond the point where resisting temptation mattered. She chomped into the apple fritter, chewing each bite into a pulp before swallowing, because mastication prevented her from thinking.

The more time that passed, the more urgently Tati felt that she needed to speak to Huck right away. Maybe *he* wasn't worried about the death threats, but it was all *she* thought about. Tati teetered between fury that he ignored her and worry that something terrible had happened to him. Either way, she felt like she'd held her breath for a week, and if she didn't exhale soon, her brain would shut down.

Tati rehearsed their conversation over and over in her mind. "Oh, hello, Huck. Has it been a week already? Well, I've uncovered some very interesting information about your case." Then, in between telling him about her interview with Detective Witt, Chavonne becoming SECSY, and the horrors Jay-Rome had witnessed in the Booti Tooti Club, she would slip in a subtle declaration of "I love you."

How would he respond? In her dreams, he paused, asked her to repeat what she just said, and then, satisfied he'd heard correctly, would acknowledge in a quavering voice, "I love you too."

At that point, though, her imagined scenario collided with stark reality. In Huck's case, love truly was not enough. Love wouldn't get him out of jail. If Tati was to save him, she needed to do it with evidence. Therefore, Tati decided she would stick to the facts. Any personal declaration might confuse him. She needed to shield Huck from reality so he could do his best thinking. And she needed to shield herself from reality to keep from imagining the worst.

Tati stuffed the rest of the apple fritter into her mouth, which had the salubrious effect of making her sick. She hurried to the toilet and purged her feelings while emptying her guts. It took two flushes to dispose of everything.

When Tati returned to her room, her mother was sitting on her bed and staring at the wall. "¡Órale!" Ximena cried. "What have you done to this wall?"

For lack of anything else constructive to do, and inspired by her visit with Detective Witt, Tati had constructed her own crazy board on her bedroom wall.

Instead of placing Huck's mugshot in the center with all lines converging on him, Tati had pinned a photo of him wearing academic regalia at the top, as if looking down from his ivory tower. Adjacent to but below Huck's picture was a photo Tati had taken of Detective Witt, with a curlicue mustache and devil horns drawn onto her face. Beneath were printouts from various social media postings, organized by hashtags in separate columns, with strings of thread connecting comments to their various sources, including @DGlint!, @GinnyCampbell, @MadameSECSY, @LadyMuleskinner, and others. At the very bottom of the wall, she had drawn a gender-neutral silhouette of a head shot, with #KillERB? written above it.

Tati stood with her back to the crazy board and extended her arms, as if trying to conceal it. "Nothing."

"It looks to me like something more than *nada*. Let me see."

Tati inched aside when her mother stepped forward. Watching Ximena review the evidence filled Tati with uneasiness, as if each item on the board revealed a secret. After all, her mother had repeatedly advised Tati not to obsess over Huck's case—although Tati felt like if she didn't obsess, she wasn't trying hard enough.

When Ximena finished her examination, she asked, "You did all of this?"

"It's nothing, really."

"*¡Deja de hablar!* Tati, this is *extraordinario*. I don't know what it all means, but I'm impressed. This looks just like something from the Policía Federal Ministerial."

Tati played those words over again in her head. "Really. Do you think so?"

"*Si, si, si.* You are a regular *federale*. Have you told this to Huck yet?"

"I was worried Huck might think this is dumb," Tati confessed.

"Dumb?" Ximena scoffed. "When I worked with Huck, he used to come to Drip 'n' Donuts with a different shoe on each foot and his shirt buttoned wrong. Huck *is* very smart. *¡Es verdad!* But about practical matters, he is dumber than a—how they say?—bag of rocks."

Ximena threw open her arms, tossed back her head, and exclaimed, "*¡Amor de lejos, amor de pendejos!*"

"Mother! What did you call me?"

Ximena sat on the bed and patted the mattress for Tati to sit next to her. "Listen to me," she said. "If Huck isn't looking for something, he won't see it, even if it is right in front of his nose."

Tati laughed into her hand. "Do you think I should call him?"

Ximena lifted Tati's head by the chin so she couldn't look away. "Tati, I only mean that love makes a girl stupid. And love from a distance is the stupidest kind. So, no, I do not think you should call him on the telephone."

Tati cried, "Really?"

"I think that you should drive to see him, right now." Ximena bounced onto her feet and began pulling down materials from Tati's crazy board. "And take all of these things with you. *¡Vamos¡*"

While growing up on the Carp family farm, Huck's sole responsibility had been tending the sheep. His brothers teased that it was the only chore he was incapable of screwing up, and although he resented their saying so, their contention was largely true, because sheep required minimal care. This arrangement suited Huck, for although he pretended his brothers' disrespect offended him, it quietly pleased him to leave them all the hard and/or disgusting work. Huck didn't mind they thought he was a laggard if that meant he'd never have to reach into a cow's rear end.

Huck first got the idea that he wanted to be a sociologist from observing sheep. They were compulsively social animals, surrounding themselves with the safety and security of the flock. Theirs was an essentially leaderless society, operating under the aegis of group conscience, for not even the bellwether could impose his will upon the masses. Apart from rams during rutting season, they were docile. Above all, they followed. They were programmed for compliance and submission. If one animal broke from the others for any reason, they would pursue it en masse, over a cliff if that's where it led. On their own, they did dumb things, like get their heads stuck in wire fences or step into cattle guards. Nothing was more desperate or terrified than a sheep separated from its flock.

Even though Huck knew he had it easy, his disdain for farm life likewise began with sheep. The urine smell of their stalls burned his sinuses. They squirmed like they were being tortured whenever Huck tried to shear them. No matter how frequently he trimmed their hooves, they still stomped in their own shit and got foot rot. Their bleating sounded like a cross between weeping and vomiting, and it made his stomach clench to hear them. Given his druthers, Huck would have never crossed paths with another sheep again in his life.

Nevertheless, his mother put him to work feeding the sheep while he bided his time on the farm. "You gottsa earn your keep," she said to him on the first day home.

"How?"

"You-uh feed sheep. Like when you-uh young boy."

Huck made a prune face. "Really?"

"Yah. Really so."

"I'm busy, Mother," he argued.

"You-uh always busy but you-uh never do nothing!" she remarked.

Actually, that was an astute observation. From most people's point of view, a scholar didn't do anything at all. Thinking deeply is often misconstrued as laziness.

"How about I do your taxes instead?" Huck counteroffered. "I could probably save you money."

"If I can't trust you-uh to feed sheep, how can I trust you-uh to do my taxes?"

That seemed a harsh expression of how little confidence she had in him. So, he set out to prove her wrong—he would feed those goddamned sheep, and he'd do it without being asked. Afterwards, he'd do her taxes, too.

Since sheep ate constantly, he had to distribute hay to their hoop house several times a day. One morning, while the temperature outside was just at the threshold of freezing, Huck draped himself in a heavy raincoat and drove the tractor through half rain / half snow to feed those loathsome beasts. Per usual, Elvis Pigsley followed beside the trailer and gobbled up loose bunches of hay that slipped off the flatbed. Huck had just finished unloading and was standing under the canopy of the hoop house, watching the sheep bump and bustle with each other to eat, when he heard behind him a snort and "soooooooeeeeeey."

"Shut up, you filthy swine," he yelled over his shoulder.

Giggles answered him. He turned and saw his mother, one hand holding an umbrella, the other in front of her face, pressing her index finger against the top of her nose to look like a hog's snout.

"Ha! I gottsa you a good one," his mother laughed.

Huck couldn't decide to be amused or offended, so he settled on bewildered. "Mother, what are you doing out here in the cold and rain?"

"I watch you-uh feed the sheep," she replied.

"Huh? What? Why?"

"You-uh doing a good job, yaaah," she said. "I just want to say it's so."

Huck felt her praise tingle down his spine. Coming from his mother, this was as good as a positive peer review. "Thanks."

The moment immediately passed and left them awkward in each other's company. Huck was glad when a honking car horn distracted them.

Tati, driving her mother's Honda Civic, rolled down the vehicle's window and waved as she pulled into the dirt driveway.

Huck's mother said, "Your girlfriend, she coming here."

Tati stepped into a puddle when she got out of the car, drenching her thigh-high zippered faux leather boots in an ooze of shit, suck mud, and motor oil. She wobbled on her heels and had to pull on the car door to pry herself loose. Meanwhile, a gust tangled her hair, and when she raked it away from her eyes, her beret flew off and spun across the pasture. *This isn't off to a good start*, she thought.

The beret spiraled toward Huck, who stopped it by stomping on it. He picked it up, looked at the damage, and tried to fluff it by rolling his fist inside of the headband. As if to bring it back to life, he blew on it.

As Tati plodded across the pasture toward Huck, she passed his mother heading back toward the house. She smiled at Tati and said, "I am glad for you-uh coming."

"Thank you. How's Huck?"

Without stopping, she nodded toward him, as if to say *see for yourself.* "I hope you-uh have some of the good news."

"I do too," she replied, then they continued in opposite directions.

Huck cleared his throat and handed the muddy, flattened beret to Tati. They stood across from each other for an intensely awkward moment before Tati said, "Thank you." Although, she would've preferred for him to lead with, "I'm sorry," or something to at least acknowledge that the beret she bought hoping he would like it now looked like a soggy felt pancake.

One of the sheep looked up from eating and bleated, thereby provoking a cacophony of *baaaaa-ing* and *meeeeh-ing*. Elvis Pigsley snorted. It sounded to Tati like the barnyard animals mocked her.

Huck turned and yelled at them, "Shut up!"

To Tati's astonishment, the beasts complied. "I'm impressed," she said. "They actually listen to you."

"That's only because I feed them," he explained.

"Oh? So, you're like their shepherd?"

Something about her question amused Huck, and when he laughed, Tati did too, so it became a spontaneous, private joke between them.

Regaining his composure, Huck sputtered, "I, uhm, was going to call you."

"I know. But I have so much to tell you that I decided to come."

"Well, let's go inside, where we can talk."

Hopping onto the tractor seat, Huck scooched over to make room for her. Tati sat pressing hips and shoulders against him. Even though four layers of clothing separated them, including his wool-lined raincoat and her puffer jacket, Tati felt a thrill. They bounced as Huck drove to the barn. It was sort of arousing, although Tati fought back those feelings by watching the hog follow them. Once inside the barn, Huck slid off the seat and offered his hand to help her down. Tati removed her gloves and accepted his gracious assistance. The hog retreated to its wallow.

Huck led Tati into the house, where they disrobed their winter coats, hats, gloves, and boots, leaving everything in the foyer. Huck even took off his wet socks. Tati had never seen his bare feet—he had the smoothest, most svelte arches she'd ever imagined. She wondered what his toes tasted like.

Tati rolled down her socks, slid them over her heels, and freed her toes one at a time. It felt liberating.

"Let's go to my room," Huck said. "We can talk there."

Huck hadn't made his bed. He smoothed a section of the comforter and invited her to sit next to him. Legs dangling over the side of the bed, they brushed ankles. If Huck so much as winked at her, she wouldn't refrain from rolling on top of him.

"So. What do you have for me?"

What do you want, she thought, but said, "Huh?"

"The investigation."

"Oh, yeah. Right."

Huck faced her. The mattress sagged between them. "So?"

Get a grip, Tati said to herself as she sank closer to him. *No, not that kind of a grip!!!* She closed her eyes and held them shut. "I went to that detective and betrayed you, just like you asked."

"Tell me what happened."

"When I asked for a glass of water, she left me alone in the office for a minute. I took pictures." Tati removed the cell phone from her back pocket. "Here, this is a picture of the board where she posted all of the evidence."

Huck lifted her palm so he could look at the phone with her. His eyes darted back and forth. "What else?"

"Here's a picture I took of her computer screen. She was looking at Twitter, with a window open to the hashtag #PutERBtoBedWet.

"Interesting," Huck said.

"I took more pictures in her office, too. The next one is her desk, and here's another that shows inside her desk drawer."

"Interesting," Huck repeated.

Tati kept talking without acknowledging his comments—or lack thereof. "I gave her that file. What were those articles about, anyway?"

"They were theoretical."

"She said she'd turn them over to the research department."

"What else did she say?"

Tati thought for a moment—not to recall, but to decide if she wanted to say it aloud. "She said all men are pigs."

"Ha," Huck chuckled. "That's an insult to swine."

"Ha." Tati also laughed, wondering why that was funny. "I recorded the whole meeting on my cell phone."

Tati played the audio. Huck balled his fist under his chin while listening. He commented "interesting" several times. When it was finished, he said, "You did a great job. This helps me a lot."

Tati danced on the inside, but apart from curling her toes, she maintained her equanimity. "I'm just glad I could help," she said. "But there's more."

"Oh?"

"Yes. It was a team effort. Jay-Rome went back to that titty bar, and discovered... well, it's kind of gross. And Chavonne got into SECS. I copied everything they sent to her."

Huck lifted his legs onto the bed leaned his back against the headboard. "Tell me. Leave out not a single detail."

And Tati, sitting next to him on his bed, his bare feet next to her bare feet, told him everything she knew.

"We need to get out of here," Huck said when Tati finished speaking. He sprang out of bed and rummaged through his socks drawer, pulling out a pair of mismatched argyles.

"Really, Huck?" Tati bumped his hands out of the way and fished through the drawer for a coordinated pair, suitable for wearing in public. "Try these."

Thanks," Huck said. He put them on, hopping one leg at a time, then slipped into a pair of suede loafers. "Let's go."

"Where are we going?" Tati asked.

"I need to get onto the Internet."

They dashed out of the room, past Huck's mother, who was washing dishes.

"Where you-uh are going?" she asked.

Tati answered, "He needs to get on the Internet."

"True that," Huck concurred, then added, "So I can solve this mystery."

His mother took her rubber-gloved hands out of the dishwater and shooed them along. "Yaaah," she said. "But bundle up, do, because it's cold out the side."

CHAPTER 13

Sally Witt sat at her desk, sipped coffee, and mulled over the crazy board. She had spent hours staring at it, but rather than reinforcing her confidence that she'd gotten the right culprit, its constancy made her skittish. She really wanted for Huck Carp to be guilty. He thought he was too smart to get caught. None of his fancy-assed words or pseudo-intellectual bullshit masked the fact that he had means and motive to kill Adam Erb, no alibi, and was caught red-handed tampering with evidence. It seemed like an open-and-shut case. The problem was there were no problems — no loose ends, false leads, unanswered questions, or unresolved issues. The evidence didn't settle well in her gut, like jello — solid going down, but dissipating into liquid in her stomach.

Out of the corner of her eye, Sally noticed that the Internet, which had been frozen all morning, suddenly flared back to life on her computer screen. Numerous postings paraded across the monitor, most containing the same short message, which multiple contacts had posted, reposted, and forwarded to several social media sites: *Adam Erb's killer unveiled! #MurdERBsolved.*

It originated from @HuckCarp. Damn him — he was supposed to be beyond the reach of the Internet. It almost seemed like he sent the message in direct response to her doubts.

Just then, the captain entered Detective Witt's office. He wore such a sour expression on his face that she withheld her typical "Good morning, captain," and went directly to "What's the matter, captain?"

"We just got a ping on your boy Huck's ankle monitor. He's on the move."

Her boy? It sounded to Detective Witt like the captain blamed her.

"Shit! What's that little weasel up to now?"

"At this very moment, he's driving south on Route Three, heading toward the city. I want you to go bring him in. Now!"

Detective Witt turned off her computer. "Will do, captain. I got a pretty good hunch about where he's going."

Chavonne followed Huck's progress via his tweets. He wasn't being coy about his intentions. His first tweet read: *Returning to the scene of the crime. #MurdERBsolved.* As a courtesy, Huck emailed Chavonne from the road to tell her he was coming. "I apologize for any inconvenience," he wrote.

What he euphemistically referred to as "any inconvenience," however, quickly devolved into hordes of devoted ERB-ites, furious ERBonians, assimilated ERBoids, academic ERBologists, starstruck ERBophiliacs, and desperate ERBoholics assembling in the parking lot outside of Drip 'n' Donuts, eagerly awaiting Huck's arrival and the promised resolution of the murder of Adam Erb.

Then, thanks to Val, who enthusiastically reposted all messages to her followers, this ultimate ERB hashtag skyrocketed to the top of the local trends list. Within half an hour of leaving the farm, Huck had engineered an online chain reaction that reached every soul with a computer or cell phone within the greater Columbus metropolitan area. Furthermore, Huck's postings en route lured fanatics, rubberneckers, and sensation mongers onto the road, so a growing entourage followed him and Tati as they headed toward Columbus. By the time the police caught up to them, the convoy had grown large enough to block every lane of southbound traffic. In addition to the police cruisers, the WXOF and WCBN media vans fell into the logjam and proceeded along with everybody else in an OJ-esque slow roll, bound for the Cleveland Avenue Drip 'n' Donuts.

The scene outside the donut shop reminded Chavonne of a dude she'd once dated named Clarence Bone, who took her to a rave party in the vacant Lazarus store in the desolate old Eastland Mall. That scene was a SWAT raid waiting to happen—loud, overcrowded, illegally occupied, and permeated with the fog of marijuana. Soon after they entered, Chavonne dispatched Clarence to fetch her a drink, then took the opportunity to escape. She stole away behind doors marked Staff Only and made her way to the food court, where she watched and waited for the shit to hit the fan.

It was just after midnight when overwhelming police forces arrived in cruisers with sirens blaring. Cop helicopters bathed the premises in searchlights. With blitzkrieg precision, they indiscriminately corralled partygoers and herded them into waiting transit vans, equally unmoved by pleas for mercy or accusations of police brutality. The gawkers and bystanders that spilled out from the neighboring apartments very quickly outnumbered the police, which added to the tension. The cops separated Clarence Bone from the others, cuffed him, read him his rights, and then shoved him into the back of an unmarked vehicle. From her hiding place, Chavonne watched dazed and aghast by the mob drama, but grateful she had avoided getting swept up in the melee.

The pandemonium breaking out around Drip 'n' Donuts made Chavonne think of that night. From her office, she watched bystanders clog the sidewalks, like cattle in a chute, while car after car turned off Cleveland Avenue into the parking lot. Her first impulse was to flee to someplace where she could watch at a safe distance. This time, however, absconding was not an option. This was her turf. She had to protect it.

Chavonne couldn't control the masses congregating in the parking lot, but she damn sure could manage whom she permitted to enter the store. People had packed the shop and were milling about when she burst out of her office and ordered, "Everyone out!" When nobody budged, she grabbed a rolling pin and waved it menacingly. "*Now!!!*"

Chavonne herded the droves toward the door, swatting people's backsides with the rolling pin to hasten their retreat. While rounding up the interlopers, Chavonne passed Barb Knoop, who had planted herself next to the condiments bar, her arms folded as if defying anybody to move her. With a nod, Chavonne indicated she could stay. Otherwise, Chavonne only permitted staff to remain in the shop. For some reason, it seemed important to keep the drive-thru open for business. Having expelled the last of the lingerers from the premises, Chavonne closed the door and pressed her face against the glass, panting to catch her breath. The crowd outside turned its attention to southbound traffic on Cleveland Avenue, in anticipation that Huck's motorcade would soon come into view.

Standing out amid the clutter, Chavonne noticed a pewter Hummer limousine with darkened windows idling in a bus pullout. It looked like LeBron James's ride—she'd seen photos of it. So when the driver's door opened and Jay-Rome stepped out, Chavonne rubbed her eyes in disbelief. She wondered if he could introduce her to King James, if in fact that happened to be whom he was driving around in that rad buggy.

Cracking the door, she hollered at him, "Get on over here."

Jay-Rome leaned into the limo and said something to its passenger, then jogged across the street and into the shop.

Approaching from the wrong direction in a one-way alley, Tank Turner drove his muddy, jacked-up Jeep Wrangler Rubicon. He parked in front of an overflowing dumpster and hopped out, then ran around to the other side to help a woman down. Chavonne recognized her from Booti Tooti Club flyers taped inside stalls in the men's room.

"Git yo' selves in here," she called to them.

Flashing lights atop police cars, honking horns, and the hubbub of hundreds of voices heralded the arrival of Huck's motorcade. At the front of the pack, Chavonne could make out Ximena Gonsalves's Honda Civic, driven by Tati, with Huck sitting next to her, eyes glued to his cell phone. Crowds filling the streets parted to let them through.

Chavonne's cell phone rang with an incoming video call. It was Val Vargas.

"Hey, girl," Val called out to Chavonne when she answered. "Can I ask a big favor? Could you hold up your cell phone so I can see what's happening? I'm going to livestream everything."

"Yeah. I'll fix yo' up," Chavonne answered.

"This is going to be historic," Val exalted.

"That's what I'm afraid of," Chavonne replied.

"Everything will be alright," Huck reassured Tati. She looked terrified.

"That's what everybody always says before things turn to shit," Tati replied. Her hands were fused like claws to the steering wheel, her knuckles white and trembling. During the last few miles of their slow transport, she'd driven in a near-catatonic state, silent, staring at the road ahead, as if blanking out the spectacle of cop cars and media vans following them, and citizens lining the curbs along their route. Her leg was shaking; to soothe her, Huck placed a hand on her knee.

The last quarter mile felt interminable. Their car inched through the crowd, while people pressed their faces against its windows, banged on its sides, and tried to ride on its hood. Huck waved at them. As vehicles in the convoy pulled over to park, the police cars and the media vans from the WXOF and WCBN mobile-broadcast teams advanced until they lined up behind the car's bumper. Finally, upon reaching Drip 'n' Donuts, Tati pulled into a handicapped space—an affront that normally Huck would have denounced, but which seemed permissible under the circumstances.

Huck pried Tati's fingers from the steering wheel one by one. She opened her mouth to speak, but only dry air came out.

"Let me do the talking," he said to her.

At the forefront of a phalanx of police officers, Detective Sally Witt bounced heel to toe, handcuffs glistening. "Hyun-ki Carp, you are under arrest for violating the conditions of your bail, refusing to stop for a police officer, inciting to riot— and that's just the start," the detective barked at him.

Huck looked left to D'Nisha Glint and the WCBN camera, to the right and Ginny Campbell and the WXOF camera. Inside the shop, Chavonne stood behind the glass door and held her cell phone with the screen facing out, where Huck could just see Val Vargas's face peer back at him.

"I have solved the murder of Adam Erb," Huck called out for the crowd to hear.

"Shut up," Detective Witt growled, pulling his hands out of his pockets to snap them into the handcuffs.

"Hear me out, Detective Witt," Huck said, projecting his voice loud enough so the crowd could hear. "Or, should I call you Lady Muleskinner?"

Sally dropped the handcuffs.

The captain, who'd met her at the scene, bent over, picked them up, and handed them to her. "What's he talking about, detective?"

"Good morning, captain," she said. "Don't listen to him. He doesn't know what he's talking about."

"Oh, but I do!" Huck shouted, egging on the crowd. They responded with cheers and an emerging chant of "Huck, Huck, Huck." He bowed to them before turning to the detective and her captain. "Let's go inside, and I'll tell you who killed Adam Erb."

The captain rubbed his chin as he looked around at the crowd. "I agree," he said. "Let's get out of public view."

Detective Witt ground her teeth.

Huck pointed to D'Nisha Glint. "You should come too." He then pivoted and said the same thing to Ginny Campbell. Chavonne held the door open and reminded everybody to wipe their feet before entering. The last inside was Tati, to whom Chavonne gave a big hug and a kiss on the forehead.

"Yo' momma has been worried sick," she said.

Once everybody was inside, Huck watched his guests arrange themselves into their respective social units. The whole time, customers continued placing orders at the drive-thru.

Detective Witt and the captain stood side by side, arms crossed, and their backs to the soft drinks fountain.

D'Nisha Glint checked out her reflection in the glossy side of the TurboChef oven, while her camera dude — Abelard, was that his name? — tapped on a microphone, saying, "Testing." Ginny Campbell commandeered a booth, while Troll, with his camera on his shoulder, munched a french cruller.

Tank sat in a wire chair next to a round bistro-style table, with Nadine L'Amour on his lap. Jay-Rome, in his chauffeur's uniform, stood behind the counter and helped himself to coffee and a devil's food donut. Barb Knoop stood alone, as far away from everybody else as she could get and still be in the same room.

Tati and Chavonne sat side by side on counter stools; they cast one long merged shadow.

"Hellllll-o, Huck," Val's voice trilled through Chavonne's cell phone, which was propped against a sugar dispenser on the counter. Her head was too large to fit in the screen, so her brow and chin were cut off. "I'm here too."

"I always assume you are everywhere," Huck assured her.

The setting suited Huck. He positioned himself in front of the pastry display case, framing himself with donuts. The disquiet in the air reminded Huck of the first day of class, when he entered the lecture hall by slowly walking down its central aisle, then stood alone before rows and rows of undergraduates assembled for Sociology 101, all hanging in suspense for his next words.

Clearing his throat, Huck summoned his most stentorian professorial voice. "Adam Erb's killer is among us here today."

In her lonely corner of the room, Barb Knoop clutched her heart and moaned.

Huck continued. "It took me awhile to piece together all of the clues. In that regard, I thank my research team—Tati, Chavonne, Jay-Rome, and you, too, Val—for gathering facts I could not have found on my own."

Chavonne gave herself a round of applause. Jay-Rome saluted. Val blew a kiss. And Tati lifted her head, her eyes brimming with gratitude, a tear trickling down her cheek.

"At first, I took a conventional approach to this homicide investigation. Premeditated murder is personal, usually the solitary act of one troubled person, often with a grudge against the victim. So, I asked myself—who had the strongest motive to kill Adam Erb?"

Huck slowly scanned the faces in front of him, then stopped when he got to Barb Knoop.

"I think that you, Barb, may be the person here who has the most conflicted emotions toward Adam. It's possible you loved him. It's also possible you wanted him dead. Those emotions are not mutually exclusive."

"No!" Barb objected.

"No? Maybe so. But it's still likely you resented him, for any of a host of reasons—because he lied to you, because he took advantage of you, because he ditched you, and because he never returned your calls, even though he left you carrying his child. That's reason enough to want to kill him."

"I didn't kill him. I loved that asshole," Barb said in an achy voice.

"Exactly!" Huck jabbed his index finger in the air. "Adam Erb was a shameless womanizer, but you knew that. In fact, knowing that made you feel special, because he chose *you* from all the other women available to him in Daisy Mae's Moonshiner Tavern. That was enough to pass for love, at least for a night, am I right?"

"If you got to ask, then you'll never understand," Barb said.

"No, I don't understand, thankfully." Huck drummed his fingers on a tray of cinnamon buns. "But if not for love—no matter how misguided—perhaps you killed him for money. It surely occurred to you that having his child gave you claim to a large piece of his estate. His death could make you millions."

"I ain't saying I wouldn't take his money," Barb snapped, becoming defensive. "But I preferred both, him *and* his money. He would have taken care of me. I believe that's so."

"Doubtless, Adam would have paid you off, just like he did many other women. Whether he would have *taken care* of you, emotionally, is dubious, but also a moot point. What matters is that you gave him the benefit of the doubt, so it's reasonable to assume you truly did want him to live."

Huck drew an X in the air, as if crossing Barb off an invisible list of suspects.

He continued, "I examined all potential motives for murdering Adam — love, hatred, sex, money, jealousy, passion, et cetera — and I considered the garish way he was killed and how the body was presented, and I came to realize that the murder was for show. Adam was a celebrity first, a real human being second. I don't think the murder was personal; it was business."

Detective Witt complained, "What in the hell do you mean, it wasn't personal? He wasn't just murdered. His body was fucking desecrated. If that ain't personal, I don't know what is."

"Thank you for making my point," Huck said. "If this were a class, I'd give you extra credit."

Detective Witt snorted and fumed; the captain held her back.

"Sociologically speaking, this was a very sophisticated murder. The killer wanted to disgrace and humiliate Adam Erb, that's true. But not for personal satisfaction. Rather, the whole point was to manufacture a public spectacle that would elicit a wide range of emotions, including shock, disgust, outrage, grief, fear, sadness, anxiety, and even joy. The killer staged Adam's body to stimulate intergroup confrontation between various normative value systems, using reflexive control techniques to manipulate diverse and conflicting feelings between convergent ideologies, creating a continuous feedback loop." Huck paused to allow the brilliance of his hypothesis to settle in.

Judging from the blank expressions on their faces, though, Sally Witt spoke for the group when she asked, "What kind of academic bullshit are you feeding us?"

Huck sighed. "If you'd read those articles that I sent you, Detective Witt, you'd understand."

Tati spoke up, "Maybe, Huck, you could explain it to them the way you did to me."

Huck nodded to her, then turned to the others. "Never underestimate the power of gossip," he said. "The murderer wanted to create a crime scene that would get everybody talking. And it worked like a charm."

"Why for?" Detective Witt demanded.

"One obvious reason is for attention—as in, television ratings. Am I right, Ms. Glint? Ms. Campbell?"

D'Nisha made a crisscross gesture with her arms, conveying to the camera dude to stop filming. "What are you implying?" she asked indignantly.

Ginny cringed and stiffened in her chair, while next to her, Troll stopped chewing. "That might be something *she* would do"—Ginny alleged, pointing at D'Nisha—"but not me. I liked Adam!"

"Bitch!" D'Nisha cried. She rushed toward Ginny, leading with her fingernails. Ginny turned over the table and shielded herself behind it.

Detective Witt restrained D'Nisha by wrapping her arms around her. Ginny stuck out her tongue and wagged her hands next to her ears.

"Break it up, or I will arrest you both and put you in the same cell," Detective Witt warned.

"She wouldn't last ten seconds," D'Nisha sneered.

"Neither would your plastic surgery," Ginny returned.

Huck gestured for a timeout. "Please, ladies. I don't believe either of you killed Adam Erb just for ratings."

"Of course, that's preposterous," Ginny said.

"Not only that, it's insulting," D'Nisha fumed.

"It's neither," Huck said, then added, "But you, Ms. Glint, are too vain to dirty your hands with the messy business of murder."

"I am not!" D'Nisha cried, then thought about it a second longer. "Uh, never mind."

Huck ignored her. "And you, Ms. Campbell, are more a manipulator than a murderer."

"That's right," Ginny concurred. "Uh, never mind."

"On the other hand, his death did serve both your interests. So, I considered the possibility that the two of you collaborated to kill him."

Ginny and D'Nisha exchanged silent, shocked looks. Troll burped softly.

Huck elaborated. "Each of you has a particular audience. Ms. Glint appeals to those who hate Adam Erb, and Ms. Campbell caters to those who love him. Those two audiences seldom interact. But by working together, despite frankly despising each other, you both could stoke and provoke your own followers and, ironically, both benefit from inflaming passions against each other. With Adam Erb dead, you could tweak your followers so both your ratings would go through the roof, and the best part is, you could keep right on hating each other."

D'Nisha stomped her feet. "I'd die before I'd kill somebody with her!"

Ginny peeked over the top of the overturned table. "Ditto."

Huck took a long breath, then continued. "But I came to realize that I wasn't thinking big enough. There was more at stake than just television ratings. The murder of Adam Erb was a much bigger sensation on the Internet than just on television. When I examined the trends he inspired on the Internet, I saw he inflamed not only passions, but also passionate ambivalence."

"Huh?" Detective Witt asked. "Are you saying people loved not knowing how they felt about him?"

"Precisely. At first, he rose to fame as a hero of the millennial professional metrosexual class of Columbus. He was a stupendously successful businessman, as well as a thinking-person's sex symbol. Then, when women came forward with tawdry allegations about his conduct, the gentrified classes turned against him. A playboy was chic, but a sexist was a pariah.

"At about the same time, though, he found new support from blue-collar working men and women—especially women. He pandered to them with his *Talking Truth* podcast. So, some people loved him, then hated him, and some people hated him only to love him in the end."

"That's awfully confusing," Detective Witt said.

"Yes, it is. But it's true. Many people loved some things about him and hated other things. There was a hidden demographic of undecideds, who didn't know exactly how they felt about Adam Erb but wanted to join the conversation, nevertheless. These people found their niche on the Internet." Huck pointed at Sally Witt. "Like Lady Muleskinner."

"What? Why? How did you know?" she stammered.

"I had a hunch, detective. I knew you were the lead investigator on Adam's sexual misconduct case, but you never got the chance to finish it when the women withdrew their complaints. That frustrated you. You wanted to get back at him. But then he started *Talking Truth*. You heard it and, despite yourself, agreed with what he said. Hence, I concluded you were passionately ambivalent about Adam Erb.

"Still, I wasn't certain you were Lady Muleskinner until I listened to the recording that Tati made when she met with you in your office."

"Huh?" Detective Witt shot Tati a laser stare.

Tati shrugged at her and mouthed, "Sorry."

"Once I heard you say, 'good morning, captain,' I recalled the opening line of the old country song, 'Muleskinner Blues.' I grew up in Knox County, where that song is practically an anthem. Also, one of the most popular versions was sung by Tennessee Ernie Ford, who is also credited with the expression, "rode hard and put to bed wet," which means putting a horse to stable without brushing and grooming it properly afterwards, although, obviously, the phrase also has sexual connotations, if you think that way. All of that, plus the fact Tati discovered your bottom desk drawer was full of cowboy romance novels, just like the ones placed in stacks at the Erb memorial behind Drip 'n' Donuts, led me to conclude that you are Lady Muleskinner."

"So what?" Sally griped. "Ain't a crime."

"No. Not at all. I merely wanted to point out that your hashtag, #PutERBtoBedWet started a massive social media trend, even though nobody quite knew what it meant. People could read into it whatever fantasy suited them. And so could you."

Huck brushed aside Sally Witt's dumbfounded expression and continued, "But Lady Muleskinner wasn't the only trendsetter who touched a nerve with the passionately ambivalent people of Columbus. Another was Madame Secsy." Huck put his hands together, palms up in a giving gesture, and turned to Tank and Nadine. "I believe the two of you are acquainted with her, aren't you?"

"I don't know no Madame Slippery, or whatever you called her," Tank insisted.

"I do," Nadine confessed.

Tank looked at her like she was a stranger. "You do?"

"I thought you knew, silly. She's Rosie Dunne."

"Sybil Exxxotica?"

"Yeah, except she doesn't go by either of those names anymore. Now, she's Madame Secsy."

Tank whistled. "Well, I'll be stiffened. I never knowed it. What's a Madame Secsy, anyway? Does she still do the act?"

Huck jumped in to stop Nadine from answering. "If I'm not mistaken, she's outside waiting in that limo." He pointed to the Hummer idling in the bus pullout. "Isn't that right, Jay-Rome."

Jay-Rome started at the sound of his name. "I can't say," he replied. "A chauffeur is sworn to keep secret what goes on inside his limo. So, don't ask me nothing."

"How's the new job working out?" Nadine asked.

"Very fine, Ms. Nadine. Thank you for the reference."

"Glad to do it for a good customer."

"And after driving Adam Erb for so long, it's sure 'nuff good to finally have a boss that respects me."

Huck rapped against the wall to regain everybody's attention. "Her identity is irrelevant. The important thing is that Madame Secsy knew Adam Erb. Very well, indeed."

"Did Adam sleep with Madame Secsy?" D'Nisha blurted out.

"That's so huge!" Ginny seconded.

"No, no, no. That's the problem. Adam Erb wanted to sleep with her, but was unable to perform. He saw her dancing one night at the Booti Tooti Club, back when she was still Rosie Dunne—errr, Sybil Exxxotica. After the show, he invited her into his limousine for a private show. Isn't that right, Jay-Rome?"

"I can't say," Jay-Rome repeated.

"You don't have to," Huck said. "It's obvious, when you consider the facts. On that night when you drove Adam to the Booti Tooti Club, he brought a large-breasted woman back to the limousine with him. None of this was unusual, except, probably, you wondered what was going on back there when you smelled cigar smoke. Suddenly, Ms. Exxxotica fled the vehicle in an agitated state. Perhaps she was upset, or perhaps she was excited, you couldn't tell—but either way, you knew something was wrong. When you went to check on Adam, he was distraught and didn't want to talk. I needed to find out what happened, though, so I asked you to go to the Booti Tooti Club yourself. When you told me about the, uh, particularly unique, uh, brand of burlesque Ms. Nadine practices in the back room there, I put the pieces together. When Adam watched Ms. Exxxotica's act in the back of his limo that night, he suffered from traumatic erectile dysfunction."

"Our act does have that effect on some men," Nadine admitted.

"Not on me," Tank was quick to point out.

"Good for both of you," Huck congratulated them, then continued. "This was of course very disheartening to Adam, not only because he was embarrassed, but because he had a reputation to protect. So, like Adam did with many other women who kept his secrets, he paid off Ms. Exxxotica with a generous settlement. She then resigned from the Booti Tooti Club and used the money to establish the Society of Enlightened Celibate Savants. From that moment, she became Madame Secsy."

"So that's what happened to her," Tank muttered. "She could've at least said goodbye."

"I'm glad for her," Nadine said. "But celibacy ain't for me."

"True. It's not for everybody," Huck concurred, then added, "But for some people, it's a viable life choice. Madame Secsy created a web page and immediately began recruiting members to the society. These days, there are a lot of sexually confused and conflicted people. She promised them a simpler life, more stable relationships, and spiritual growth. On the night he died, the last site Adam Erb visited on the Internet was the SECS page. I believe he was thinking about joining them."

"Whoa," D'Nisha exclaimed. "That's totally mind-blowing."

"That's an even bigger story than his coming up limp," Ginny opined.

Huck began to pace. "Remember, the killer staged Adam Erb's body wearing a chastity belt, which was a clear reference to SECS."

"No way," Nadine jumped in. "Call her Rosie, or Sybil, or Madame Secsy, or what have you, but she's my friend, and I know she couldn't kill nobody."

"I agree. But his death did give her organization a boost. Madame Secsy started several social media trends with her numerous #ProvERBs postings. Ever since, membership in SECS has boomed."

"I joined," Chavonne interrupted. "They don't let just anybody into the club, but if yo' pass their screening process, they make yo' feel right at home. I've done had me a date every night since joining."

Huck stood behind the cash register like a lectern. "Now, let's recapitulate," he said.

"Fact one: Adam Erb let his murderer into his house on the night he was killed. Supposition: his murderer was a woman whom he knew, and he probably expected to have sex with her. I would guess that he took a couple tablets of Viagra on his own before letting her inside his home.

"Fact two: Adam Erb's body was handcuffed and his cheeks were full of candy valentine hearts made of high-dosage Viagra. Supposition: his murderer chose Viagra as a murder weapon as much for its irony as its utter shock value. I surmise that Adam did not know what he took. Perhaps he thought her feeding him candy was foreplay, so he consented not only to that, but also to being handcuffed. Once he was bound, though, the murderer force-fed him so fast he swallowed in large gulps just to keep up, which resulted in a fatal overdose by triggering a massive cardiac infarction.

"Fact three: Adam Erb's body was staged in a grotesque and humiliating fashion. Supposition: the murderer wanted to evoke strong reactions from his friends and enemies alike. In doing so, she left clues. For example: The chastity belt was a reference to SECS, so the murderer had some connection to that organization. The body was dressed in attire that anticipated appearances on Adam's schedule for the next day, so the murderer had access to his personal calendar. The hashtag #pERBvert was written in marking pen on Adam's chest, so the murderer intended it to start a social media meme. A cigar was placed with Adam's body, and upon digging between the seats, I found a matchbook from the Booti Tooti Club, so the murderer was privy to the nature of Madame Secsy, or the former Sybil Exxxotica's act, as well as the debilitating influence it had on Adam.

"Finally, fact four: following Adam's death, Erb-related memes inundated social media. Supposition: the murderer intended to create chaos on the Internet by triggering so much traffic that trends not only endured, they grew exponentially, until they metastasized and brought down the entire Internet. It was a test, a challenge."

Huck lifted Chavonne's cell phone into his hand and spoke into it. "So, Val, do you see where I'm going with this?"

"Barnacles," Val gulped, then swallowed and rolled her eyes. "I guess yah got me, Huck."

Nobody said a word, but spoke volumes through gasps, groans, growls, and gnashing of teeth. Huck lifted the phone and showed it to the room so the others could see Val's face, and she could see theirs.

"Oh, corn nuts! Why all the gloomy faces?" Val asked.

"Say it isn't so," Tati implored.

Val twirled her hair. "My bad."

Huck questioned her further. "When you went to his home that night, two days before Valentine's Day, did you intend to kill him, or just to humiliate him, and it got out of hand?"

"Well, duh, of course Adam had to die for my plan to work. But he died happy, right until the end. He was perfectly okay indulging my fetishes, even with the handcuffs, although he definitely did not like it when I strapped on the chastity belt. After he'd eaten so much of my boner candy, getting it on him was like trying to smash a really tightly wound spring into a jack in the box. It kept popping out. I finally had to use a hammer."

Every man in the room cringed, except Huck, who persisted with, "By posing him in a chastity belt, you were making a statement, weren't you? It was a message to Madame Secsy, wasn't it?"

"That bitch!" Val swore.

"You were angry at her, weren't you? Tati noticed you were not listed in the SECS member directory, although you told us you belonged. That was a lie. You applied to join, but were refused. Isn't that right?"

"It wasn't fair," Val complained. "I haven't had sex for five years, so I'm already happily living like a celibate. But when I filled out the application, I happened to mention that I love dicks. Well, I do, but not for sex. I think of them like little pets that dudes have between their legs. They're cute, sometimes floppy, sometimes feisty, and they do tricks. I love them the way I love my kitty cat, and while I pet her and cuddle with her, I sure don't want to jam her into my hoo-ha. Just the thought makes me want to puke. I tried to explain, but Madame Secsy wouldn't listen to me. She said I wasn't qualified to join her stupid cult.

"But that wasn't the worst part. When I designed Adam's web page, I hid some bots so I could monitor his Internet activity. That's how I knew he'd been checking out the SECS site. I also knew that Madame

Secsy herself reached out to him, inviting him to join. That really peed me off. I wasn't about to let that happen."

"True that. But it wasn't the main reason for killing him, was it?" Huck asked.

"C'mon, Huck. You know that's not why I put him down."

"You had a higher purpose, didn't you? You wanted to create the ultimate Internet trend, one that never died."

"Yup. Adam was the perfect catalyst. He left behind a trail of hashtags wherever he went. I had this theory that if I could merge trends, they'd share their memes, creating a domino effect. So, I amplified some trends. And I seeded others. Finally, I sent a huge dump of Adam's email to D'Nisha Glint, and when she reposted everything, that put me over the top. My plan worked better than I ever imagined. I did it, all by myself. I took down the Internet. I discovered the Vargas Zone."

Val beamed with satisfaction. On the small screen of Chavonne's cell phone, it looked like she grew a halo.

"I'm sorry I got you involved, Huck. I needed you, though. That's why I bailed you out. See, I don't really understand all of the sociology that's going on here. That stuff is waaaay too complicated for me. I need you to figure it out and write it up in those fancy journals of yours. I think there's a Nobel Prize for you in my data, and it's all yours. Good luck with it."

Huck averted his head, as if shielding himself from the implication. He stumbled backwards and nearly fell, but Tati caught him. He sought Tati's eyes, and she opened them wide enough to let him in.

"So, you see, I didn't kill Adam Erb. I made him immortal," Val said proudly.

Detective Witt strode across the shop floor and stood face-to-screen with Val. "Valerie Vargas, you are under virtual arrest for the murder of Adam Erb. You have the right—"

"Save your breath, officer. I'm already gone. Right now, I'm on a plane, and I won't tell you where I'm going, except to say that it's someplace you'll never find me." Val lifted her kitty cat, Minou, in front of her and waved its paw. "Bye now," she said, and signed off.

The image on Chavonne's cell phone broke up into fragmented pixels that swirled clockwise, like a toilet flushing, and then went completely dark. A split second later, every cell phone in the room discharged an earsplitting electronic wail before going blank. Outside, the same thing happened, and people in the crowd ducked and covered.

"She done busted down the Internet again," Chavonne said.

"She has," Huck concurred. He pressed a finger against his temple. "But now she's a fugitive—she may never log on as herself again. For Val, that's a death sentence."

Tati hooked her arm with Huck's. "I can't believe it was Val."

"In Val's thinking, she didn't murder Adam Erb," Huck said, "She sacrificed him to the Internet."

EPILOGUE

Of all the people gathered around him, the last whom Huck would have expected to break the bewildered stalemate was Ginny Campbell's cameraperson. "Whoa, people," Troll said. "That was gnarly."

Ginny snapped to and pushed past D'Nisha Glint to get to Huck. "When did you first suspect?"

D'Nisha bounced back and shouted over Ginny, "Will you do an interview?"

"Shut up!" Ginny snapped. "I was here first."

"Bite me!" D'Nisha retorted. "I'm better looking."

"Ladies, please," Huck said, stepping backwards. "I have just one comment."

They held their microphones to his mouth.

"Hi, Mom," he said.

"But—"

"Please—"

Huck sidestepped them. Both women reached to grab hold of his clothing. Tati planted her feet between them and Huck, reared back with both hands, and slapped both their cheeks at once.

"What part of no comment don't you bitches understand?" she said.

While Ginny and D'Nisha rubbed their jaws and backed away, Detective Witt skulked over to Huck and sneered, "This ain't over."

"No hard feelings," Huck said and offered to shake her hand.

Detective Witt cracked her knuckles and skulked away. Behind her, the captain sidled up to Huck and patted him on the shoulder.

"Don't call me. I'll call you," he said. He shook his head as he left, chuckling to himself, "'Rode hard and put to bed wet,' eh? That's a good one."

Meanwhile, the Drip 'n' Donuts staff members who'd been working the drive-thru window called for Chavonne to please help them, because they couldn't keep up with the incessant business. A new pay-it-forward streak had broken out. Chavonne pulled down an apron from a hook outside of her office and tossed it across the room to Barb.

"If yo' need a job, we could use us some help here," she said.

Barb tied the apron around her waist and put on a headset, telling the newbies on duty, "Let me show you how this is done."

Nadine got up from Tank's lap and pressed her face against the glass, looking outside at Madame Secsy's limousine.

"Is Rosie really in there?" she asked Jay-Rome.

"I don't 'xactly know what her name be," he replied. "I just call her boss."

"Let's go say hi to her," she said to Tank.

Tank grunted and wobbled as he got up. On his way out the door with Nadine, he called back to Huck, "You put on one hell of a show, kid. Drop by the club sometime, and Nadine will return the favor."

The mental image forming in Huck's mind dissipated when he felt a sharp pinch on his butt. Tati fired him a combustible look that made him embarrassed for what he'd been thinking.

"What's next?" she asked him.

"Good question. Technically, until I can meet with the district attorney, I'm still on house arrest. So, I guess I have to go back to the farm."

"I'm coming with you," Tati stated as if to discourage discussion. "And I'm bringing my toothbrush. Got it?"

"Huh?"

Tati inserted a finger into a belt loop on Huck's trousers. "How can you be so brilliant but so dense?"

Huck wasn't sure that was a serious question. He scoured his mind for any competing theories or alternate interpretations to explain what she meant to communicate to him. He wasn't certain, nor could he quite comprehend it, but her look and her disposition suggested she was trying to seduce him. A tingling sensation lit upon his shoulders.

"Are your intentions, like, uh, intimate?"

"Intimate?" Tati blurted out. "We've solved a murder together. You can't get any more intimate than that."

After giving that remark due consideration, Huck arrived at the evident conclusion. "True that," he said.

ABOUT THE AUTHOR

Gregg Sapp, a native Ohioan, is a Pushcart Prize-nominated writer, librarian, college teacher and academic administrator. He is the author of the "Holidazed" series of satires, each of which is centered around a different holiday. The first two novels, *Halloween from the Other Side* and *The Christmas Donut Revolution* were published in 2019 by Evolved Publishing. Previous books include *Dollarapalooza* (Switchgrass Books, 2011) and *Fresh News Straight from Heaven* (Evolved Publishing, 2018), based upon the life and folklore of Johnny Appleseed. He has published humor, poetry, and short stories in Defenestration, Waypoints, Semaphore, Kestrel, Zodiac Review, Top Shelf, Marathon Review, and been a frequent contributor to Midwestern Gothic, and others. Gregg lives in Tumwater, WA.

For more, please visit Gregg Sapp online at:
Website: www.SappGregg.net
Goodreads: Gregg Sapp
Twitter: @Sapp_Gregg
Facebook: Gregg.Sapp.1
LinkedIn: Gregg-Sapp-b515921b

WHAT'S NEXT?

Gregg is fast at work on the next book in the
"Holidazed" series, and other books will follow that,
so please stay tuned to his page at our website to
remain up to date:
www.EvolvedPub.com/GSapp

Indeed, the best way to be assured that you won't miss
important developments is to subscribe to our
newsletter here:
www.EvolvedPub.com/Newsletter

MORE FROM GREGG SAPP

Don't miss Gregg Sapp's award-winning adult tale of
an American icon, Johnny Appleseed.

FRESH NEWS STRAIGHT FROM HEAVEN

"I happen to believe that genius makes people weird," a
storyteller once said, explaining how Johnny Appleseed
could be at once so peculiar and so profound.

Between 1801 and 1812, Ohio and the Old Northwest
territory runs wild and brutal, with a fragile peace, savage
living conditions, and the laws of civilization far away.
Still, settlers stake everything they own on the chance of
building better lives for themselves in this new frontier.

John Chapman--aka Johnny Appleseed--knows this
land better than any white man. Everywhere he goes, he
shares the "Fresh News Straight from Heaven," which
he hears right from the voices of angels who chat with
him regularly. God had promised him personally that
he could build peace by growing fruit.

Convincing people of that vision, though, is no
easy task. Most folks consider him mad.

This land teems with a miscellaneous assemblage of
soldiers, scoundrels, freebooters, runaway slaves, circuit
riders, and religious cultists. Ambitious politicians, like

Aaron Burr and William Henry Harrison, dream of creating a new empire there. Meanwhile, a reformed drunkard emerges among the Shawnee as a Prophet, one who spoke with the Great Spirit, Waashaa Monetoo. Along with his brother, the war chief Tecumseh, the Prophet begins building an Indian coalition to take back their land.

Even while the tensions mount, Johnny, with angels urging him on, skates blithely through the crossfire and turmoil, spreading his message, impervious to the mockery and derision being heaped upon him. Finally, however, his faith is challenged when war breaks out in the land, leading to the bloody battle of Tippecanoe between Harrison's army and the Shawnee Prophet's warriors, and ultimately to the declaration of the War of 1812. A violent massacre near the northern Ohio town of Mansfield leaves its citizens terrified and vulnerable.

In a desperate act of faith, Johnny promises the people that he can save them. Thus, he dashes off on a midnight run, seeking to spread peace across a land on the brink of war. With so many lives at stake, Johnny must confront the ultimate test of his convictions.

MORE FROM EVOLVED PUBLISHING

We offer great books across multiple genres,
featuring high-quality editing (which we believe
is second-to-none) and fantastic covers.

As a hybrid small press, your support as loyal
readers is so important to us, and we have strived,
with tireless dedication and sheer determination,
to deliver on the promise of our motto:
QUALITY IS PRIORITY #1!

Please check out all of our great books,
which you can find at this link:
www.EvolvedPub.com/Catalog/

Thank you!

CPSIA information can be obtained
at www.ICGtesting.com
Printed in the USA
BVHW081004090321
602096BV00001B/271

9 781622 535255